THE HANGING HILL

ALSO BY CHRIS GRABENSTEIN

The Crossroads

THE
HANGING HILL

CHRIS GRABENSTEIN

Random House New York

Text copyright © 2009 by Chris Grabenstein
Jacket illustration copyright © 2009 by Scott Altmann

Visit us on the Web! www.randomhouse.com/kids

Educators and librarians, for a variety of teaching tools, visit us at
www.randomhouse.com/teachers

Library of Congress Cataloging-in-Publication Data
Grabenstein, Chris.
The Hanging Hill / Chris Grabenstein. — 1st ed.
p.   cm.
Summary: While working at a summer stock theater, eleven-year-old Zack and his stepmother encounter the ghost of one of Connecticut's most notorious criminals.
ISBN 978-0-375-84699-1 (trade) — ISBN 978-0-375-94699-8 (lib. bdg.) —
ISBN 978-0-375-84700-4 (trade pbk.) — ISBN 978-0-375-85384-5 (e-book)
[1. Ghosts—Fiction. 2. Stepmothers—Fiction. 3. Theater—Fiction.
4. Criminals—Fiction. 5. Connecticut—Fiction.] I. Title.
PZ7.G7487Han 2009
[Fic]—dc22
2008027274

Printed in the United States of America
10 9 8 7 6 5 4 3 2 1
First Edition

Random House Children's Books supports the First Amendment
and celebrates the right to read.

for Erick Tavira, Charlene Floyd,
and all the other students and tutors at
Homework Help

THE HANGING HILL

1

There's this thing about ghosts: Once you've seen one, you can basically see them all.

At least the ones that want to be seen.

At the age of eleven, Zack Jennings was learning the rules of the spirit world pretty quickly. He'd only seen his first real-live (make that "real-dead") spook maybe a month or two ago. Now they seemed to be everywhere. When he went to summer camp in the middle of July, he met the boy who'd drowned in the lake.

Back in 1973.

When he hung out at the library, he occasionally saw this pudgy woman reading over people's shoulders because she couldn't flip the pages herself anymore, what with being dead and all.

His mother had always claimed that Zack had a hyperactive imagination, but even he couldn't make this stuff up. The ghosts he saw were as real as electricity, wind, and gravity—things nobody could see but everybody knew were there.

Some called being a Ghost Seer a gift. Well, if it was,

Zack figured it was like getting a paisley-and-plaid sweater for Christmas when what you really wanted was an iPod. Seven weeks after learning he could see spirits, Zack was already tired of being special.

Being special could wear a guy out.

On the first Saturday of August, as he stepped into the brightly lit breakfast room of the Marriott extended-stay hotel near North Chester, Connecticut, it happened once again: He saw an apparition lurking near a small table in the far corner of the room.

Zack could tell: This one was a demon.

Zack and his family—his dad, his new stepmom, and his dog—were currently residing at the hotel because their house had burned down when Zack had battled the evil spirit haunting the crossroads nearby. The fire had been Zack's fault, and his allowance would be docked for the damages until he turned twenty-one. After that, Zack's dad would probably do payroll deductions. And now, here Zack was, less than twenty feet away from yet another fiend, who probably wanted to destroy some other part of Zack's life when all Zack wanted to do was grab a bowl of cereal and maybe a banana from the breakfast buffet.

Zack had come down to the lobby on his own.

His dad, who didn't believe in ghosts anyway, had gone into New York City for weekend work at his office.

His stepmom, Judy, an author, was upstairs, busily working on last-minute rewrites to *Curiosity Cat*, a new musical, based on her children's books, that was about to have its world premiere at a theater called the Hanging Hill Playhouse.

His trusty dog, Zipper, was also upstairs—snoozing between the cushions of a very comfy hotel couch.

There were other people in the breakfast room, the same ones Zack saw most mornings: Divorced Guy, Moving Family, Vacationing Family, Businessman, Other Divorced Guy.

The ghost was new.

Zack could tell that the man sitting at the table in the far corner of the breakfast room was a ghost because he was wearing old-fashioned clothes—the kind convicts in chain gangs sometimes wore in the movies. *Old* movies.

The ghost was, or had been, a hulking giant with a serious scowl carved into his watermelon-sized head. He wore a denim prison jumpsuit, loosely laced work boots, and a tin hat that looked like an upside-down spaghetti strainer with electrical cables clamped to battery posts where its legs should have been.

He'd shown up sitting in his own chair: a colossal throne made out of thick planks of rough-hewn lumber. Wide, double-holed leather belts were buckled tight across his chest, arms, and legs.

Zack suddenly realized the guy was strapped into an electric chair, the thing they used fifty years ago to execute hard-core criminals on death row in the state penitentiary.

The giant caught Zack staring.

"Pssst! Hey, kid!"

Zack pretended not to see or hear the man.

"I know you can see and hear me, kid."

So much for pretending.

"Come here. Undo these belt buckles!"

Slowly, very slowly, Zack turned his back on the ghost so he could face the breakfast buffet and make like he was picking out a banana. Behind him, he heard the sizzling sputter of sparks. He smelled ozone, like when an electrical outlet short-circuits and scorches the toaster plug. Zack whipped around just in time to see the last zig of a lightning bolt zap and *zizz* off the big guy's metal cap. Smoke wafted up from his razored scalp.

"Where's the bank?" the man in the chair demanded.

Zack didn't answer.

"Used to be a bank right here. Connecticut Building and Loan. Biggest heist of my career." Watermelon Head grinned. His teeth were the color of coffee beans. "Happiest day of my life, kid. Good times."

Zack glanced guardedly around the room. Nobody else could see or hear the ghost reminiscing about his bygone days of glory.

"Come on! Undo these straps!"

Now one of the kids in the Moving Family, a girl about six, was gawking at Zack like he was nuts. He didn't blame her. He probably looked pretty crazy: frozen in place, staring across the room at an empty table, mouth hanging open.

"Be a pal, kid! I've been stuck in this chair since 1959."

Zack didn't budge.

"You deaf? I said turn me loose!"

Zack stayed where he was.

"Oh, I get it," the trapped beast snarled. "Some kind of tough guy, hunh?"

Zack shook his head and slid his black-rimmed glasses up the bridge of his nose. He was sort of short and kind of skinny and really didn't look all that tough, even when he took off the glasses.

"Do you know who I am, kid?"

Again, Zack shook his head while the girl, the normal kid, kept gawking at him.

"Folks called me Mad Dog Murphy on account of the fact that I went bonkers here at the bank. Killed six people. Two of 'em kids! So shake a leg and unbuckle these straps! You think I want to spend eternity sitting on my keester on top of Old Sparky?"

Now a second ghost materialized directly across the table from the angry giant lashed into his sizzle seat. A woman. Zack couldn't see her face, just the back of her curly hair.

"Doll face!" Mad Dog Murphy said with a sinister smile. "What're you doin' here?"

The woman didn't say a word.

"What? Forget it, sister! I ain't leaving the kid alone!"

The woman raised both arms and the two ghosts began to disappear slowly. As they faded away, Zack heard Mad Dog Murphy's voice echoing off the walls in some kind of tunnel: "I'll be back, kid! You'll see! I'm comin' back to get you, Zack Jennings!"

All of a sudden, Zack didn't feel so hungry. How did this ghost know his name? None of the others ever did.

He decided maybe he'd skip breakfast, go back to the room, pack his suitcase.

"Are you okay?" asked the girl who had been staring at him.

"Yeah."

Now her mother was staring at him, too. "Are you sure?" the mother asked. "You look like you just saw a ghost."

Reginald Grimes sat alone in the kitchen of his sparsely furnished apartment, sipping a mug of bitter tepid coffee and flipping through the pages of his dog-eared script for *Curiosity Cat.*

Grimes was the artistic director of the Hanging Hill Playhouse. Had been for years. He was famous for his magnificently mounted musicals. Infamous for his rants against anyone who didn't work as tirelessly as he thought they should.

"Cut this," he muttered, scratching a red line through a sentence. "This, too." Another red line. "Fix this." A looping red circle.

Rehearsals for the new musical would start first thing tomorrow morning. The author, Judy Magruder Jennings, would be arriving at the theater tonight.

She'd have work to do.

The show was good as written. Nearly great.

But it would be absolutely perfect when Grimes had finished working his theatrical magic.

He flipped forward through the pages and came to a

scene in the second act. Curiosity Cat had gone missing. The two children who love him—a boy and a girl—are out in the dark alleys of a scary city, searching for their beloved pet. They fear he might be hurt or trapped.

Or worse.

Grimes read the lyrics to the children's emotional duet: *We'll never find another cat like that.*

"Just like Jinx," he muttered, remembering the sleek gray cat with the amber eyes who used to howl out in the alley just below his bedroom window when he was a child living in that horribly dark, dank place.

The Saint Ignatius Home for Boys.

The orphanage.

Grimes would sometimes sneak food from the cafeteria and smuggle it back to his room for Jinx. Perhaps a pinch of tuna fish, if there was any to be found in the nauseatingly crusted-over noodle casserole so often served for supper. Maybe an almost-empty carton of milk retrieved from the big rubber barrel where the boys dumped the scraps and trash from their trays.

He'd slink with his treasure back to his bedchamber, wait for the other boys to fall asleep, then creep over to the window, pry it open, and place Jinx's dinner outside on its filthy sill. Grimes would even try to fashion the waxy box into something resembling a bowl—even though this was extremely difficult, given his unusual deformity. Then he'd lie on his bed, the one nearest the window, and sleep with one eye open, waiting for

Jinx to spring up to the ledge, tightrope-walk over to the milk, and lap up his feast, which, of course, he always did.

Until the day he didn't.

The last carton of milk stayed outside the window for two full weeks. The sun soured it. Maggots writhed in the curdling slime. Still, Grimes would not remove the milk— hoping against hope that Jinx would return, knowing the cat would be ravenously famished, and therefore not very finicky, when it did.

Soon the rancid milk began to smell. The nuns who ran Saint Ignatius scoured the building, searching for the source of the foul odor, and found it perched outside the window near young Reginald Grimes's bed.

"It was for my friend, Jinx the cat," he told them after a prolonged interrogation. "I was attempting to feed the hungry."

Grimes hoped the nuns might forgive him, perhaps even praise him. After all, wasn't that what the Bible said to do, feed the hungry?

"Young man," Sister Beatrice, the sternest of the stern lot, had snapped at him, "that commandment does not apply to stray dogs, pigeons, or alley cats!"

Grimes was severely punished. For stealing food. For endangering the health and hygiene of everyone in the building. For misinterpreting Scripture.

Grimes pushed the *Curiosity Cat* script aside.

"Bah!" he said, rubbing his watery eyes. "Silly, emotional

sap. Going all weepy for a flea-infested feline?" He *tsked* and sounded just like Sister Beatrice.

Good.

He didn't have time for silly saccharine-soaked sentimentality.

There was a new show to put on.

He needed to: Concentrate. On. His. Work.

Still. That song. It haunted him.

We'll never find another cat like that.

It had been thirty-five years since he had last seen Jinx. The cat had been dead for three decades and more.

Still.

Reginald Grimes wished he could see Jinx again.

Wished he could hear his throaty, contented purr.

He wished he could bring that yellow-eyed cat back from the dead, because it might be nice to have at least one friend.

There was a noise at the window over the kitchen sink.

A low rumble.

A purr?

"Meow."

For an instant, maybe half an instant, Reginald Grimes saw his childhood companion. Sleek and gray. Glowing amber eyes. Jinx was perched right outside his kitchen window!

Claws out, Jinx hissed and swatted at the glass.

And then, before Grimes was even certain what he had seen, the cat was once again gone.

3

"Sorry we're so behind schedule," said Zack's step-mom, Judy.

"That's okay," said Zack. He was just glad no ghosts had shown up in the hotel suite to help them pack their bags for the three-week trip to Chatham. It was almost seven p.m. and getting dark outside. He dumped an arm-load of socks into his open suitcase. All the fuzzy balls were mismatched: red socks with blue, white with sort-of-white, ankle-striped athletic with ankle-logo sport.

"What's up with the socks?" Judy asked.

"I think I lost some in the laundry room."

"Maybe the sock gremlins got 'em!"

Zack, not really in the mood to joke about supernatural stuff, faked a pretty good chuckle anyhow.

Judy's big brown eyes lit up with a fanciful idea. She got a lot of them. In fact, she got more than anyone Zack had ever met except maybe himself. "You know, Zack, this hotel is brand-new," Judy said in her hushed story-teller voice. "So, maybe . . . just maybe . . . they built it on top of a fairy kingdom where all the wee people slumber inside stolen socks instead of sleeping bags!"

Zack played along—even though he knew there used to be a bank on this plot of ground, not a fairy kingdom. He Googled it. Mad Dog Murphy had, indeed, robbed the North Chester branch of the Connecticut Building and Loan back on August 3, 1959—the happiest day of his life.

"Of course," said Judy, "there might be a more logical explanation."

"Like what?"

"Well, they are socks, Zack. They could've grown feet and walked away."

"True," said Zack.

"They could've *run* away and joined a sock puppet circus."

Now Zack laughed for real. Judy was the only adult he knew with an imagination even crazier than his. It was probably why she was a writer. And why they got along so well.

"Maybe it was another ghost," suggested Zack, testing the waters. "A sock-lifter spirit."

Judy closed her suitcase. Studied his face. "Have you seen something, hon?"

"Nah," he lied. "Not, you know, recently. I'm just goofing around."

"You can tell me if you do."

"Okay."

"No matter what. You know that, right?"

"Yeah." He smiled, so she did, too. Zack knew he could talk to Judy about ghosts and gremlins and sock-swiping nymphs, because they both understood that the supernatural world was very, very real. In fact, they had spent some quality time there together. However, Zack didn't think this was such a hot time to let Judy know that one of Connecticut's most notorious criminals had shown up downstairs just in time for the breakfast buffet.

She had enough to worry about. *Curiosity Cat* was the first show Judy Magruder had ever written, and since it was about to be produced, live onstage, at one of the biggest, most famous summer stock theaters in all of America, she was, well, to put it mildly, *freaking out*!

Therefore, Mr. Mad Dog Murphy and his traveling companions, Old Sparky (according to the Internet, that was what people had called Connecticut's electric chair) and the curly-haired lady he called Doll Face, would remain Zack's secret.

Besides, they were about to get into a car and drive far, far away. Murphy, his chair, and his ghostly girl-friend would soon be nothing more than a distant memory, a bad dream forgotten just like the dragon-sized bee who'd been chasing you with an earsplitting buzz that was really your alarm clock telling you it was time to wake up.

"Hey! Easy, boy!"

Zipper, Zack's feisty little Jack Russell terrier, hopped up on the bed and started nuzzling his muzzle inside the suitcase, rooting around in the crannies between stacks of Zack's clothes.

"You sure those socks are clean?" Judy asked, cocking a quizzical eyebrow.

"Yep. Completely stink free."

Zipper kept digging, pawing a tunnel between some T-shirts and jeans.

"Did you pack any dog treats?" Judy asked with a laugh. "Peanut butter biscuits? Liver snaps? *Bones?*"

"Nope. Just this ball!" Zack dug out Zipper's favorite toy: a spongy ball with half its outside color chipped off. "Go get it, Zip!"

He tossed the ball across the hotel room. The dog leapt off the bed and flew after it. Zack saw his chance and slammed his suitcase shut.

It was time to hit the road.

They had a show to put on.

At seven-thirty p.m., Kelly Fagan was sitting in front of her makeup mirror in a dressing room backstage at the Hanging Hill Playhouse, getting ready for the Saturday-evening performance of *Bats in Her Belfry,* a Broadway musical from the 1950s about Dracula and the women who loved him.

The summer stock revival was a smash hit—just like all of Reginald Grimes's productions at the Hanging Hill.

The man was a genius. Dark, brooding, mysterious.

Kelly couldn't wait to introduce her famous director to her parents, who had driven all the way from Canton, Ohio, to Chatham, Connecticut, just to see her sing and dance in her first big show. She was one of the dancing bats. All the chorus girls were bats. The guys were werewolves.

She leaned in closer to the mirror. Becoming a bat involved applying a great deal of black and red greasepaint to her face, especially around the eyes.

She dabbed on a dollop of makeup and felt a chill tingle down her spine.

Goose bumps sprouted on both arms.

The pretty face smiling back at her from the mirror wasn't her own.

Kelly gasped.

The face disappeared.

"Everything okay, Kelly?"

It was Vickie, another chorus girl, who had just stepped into the dressing room.

"Yeah."

Vickie was carrying an old record album.

"What's that?" Kelly asked.

"*Bats in Her Belfry.* Original 1955 cast recording. Vinyl. Thought it might be cool to listen to it later, if, you know, we can dig up an old-fashioned record player."

"Who's she?" Kelly asked, pointing at the woman swooning in Dracula's arms on the cover.

"Kathleen Williams. She played Lucy. Sang 'Bitten and Smitten.' "

Kelly nodded.

Now she had a name to go with the face.

Kathleen Williams had been the pretty woman staring at her from inside the mirror.

At dusk, the Riverstream Hospital for the Criminally Insane loomed like a dark castle set against angry red clouds in the lowering sky.

Two olive-skinned men, both sporting bushy mustaches and tasseled red hats, ascended the steep stone steps to the main entrance of the dilapidated building.

"Tell me, Hakeem," asked one of the men, "why do we need him?"

"He is of the royal bloodline."

"We could do it ourselves!"

"No, Habib. We could not." Hakeem peered up at the weather-beaten six-story structure. In a small dormer jutting up through the crumbling slate roof, faint candlelight danced across the barred glass of a window. "Come. He waits for us."

"He knows we are coming?"

"Of course. Do you think we would be here had he not summoned us? Hurry. His time draws near."

"He is dying?"

Hakeem nodded solemnly.

"Then we *must* raise the army on our own!"

"No," said Hakeem. "There is another. An heir we have secretly supported for many years."

"Who?"

"Come. You ask far too many questions. All shall be revealed. Come."

They clambered up the final steps and passed underneath a grand fieldstone arch shrouded by the veined web of long-dead ivy.

A guard was stationed in the cavernous lobby. "State your business."

Hakeem did not recognize the young man. Typically, he dealt with a senile old sentry named Bob.

"Where is Bob?"

"Retired. State your business."

"I am Hakeem. This is my associate Habib. We are here to visit the professor."

The guard hiked up his gun belt, jangling an enormous ring of keys. "You've visited before?"

"Yes. Many times."

"You know the rules?"

"Yes."

The guard picked up a clipboard. "Go straight to his cell. Don't talk to any of the others. Stay six feet away from him at all times."

Hakeem nodded. "As I said, we know the rules."

The guard eyed him suspiciously.

"You family?"

"No."

"Friend?"

"Yes."

"Known him a long time?"

"Yes."

"So how old is he, anyway? Somebody told me he's a hundred."

"One hundred and five."

"I hear he used to be in show business. A magician."

"That is correct."

"Did he do birthday parties? That where he killed the kid?"

"Please, sir. We are in a hurry. Time is of the essence."

"Why? Your friend isn't goin' anywhere any time soon. He's chained and shackled to his wheelchair. Has been ever since 1939 when he went berserk and murdered that little girl."

"Please, sir. May we kindly proceed upstairs?"

"Sign here." He handed Hakeem the clipboard. "Be careful up there. Stick to the middle of the corridors. Stay away from the bars on the cell doors. You never know when one of these psychos might try to reach out and kill somebody new."

It was pitch-dark by the time they stuffed the last suitcase into the back of the Saab convertible.

"You know," said Judy, gesturing toward her backpack loaded down with a laptop, overflowing folders, assorted notebooks, and several heavily penciled manuscripts, "if I get busy, if Mr. Grimes wants more rewrites . . ."

"There are two kids my age in the show," said Zack, finishing the sentence for her. "So Zipper and I can hang out with them whenever they're not rehearsing. Don't worry, Mom. We'll be fine."

"Thanks," she said.

"For what?"

"Making this a little easier for me. I think I'm scared. I've never put my words in front of a live audience before. I just wrote books. Wasn't sitting there watching when people actually read 'em."

"Don't worry," said Zack, realizing he had been *so* right not to give Judy anything more to brood about today. "It'll be great."

"You're right. I'll be swell! I'll be great! Gonna have the whole world on my plate."

"Hunh?" said Zack.

"Sorry. It's a song. From *Gypsy*."

"What's *Gypsy*?"

"A Broadway musical."

"And it's about gypsies?"

"No. Not really. Even though, sometimes, they call dancers in Broadway shows gypsies because they move around so much, from show to show."

"Unh-hunh," said Zack. Sometimes the whole Broadway thing was too complicated. He'd stick to memorizing the stuff from Age of Empires III.

"Yep," said Judy, settling in behind the steering wheel, still sounding nervous. "There's no business like show business like no business I know."

"Really?" said Zack. "What about making widgets?"

"Nope."

"Refrigerator repair?"

"Hardly."

"Monkey business?"

"Close." Judy laughed and cranked the ignition. "You'll see. Next stop—the Hanging Hill Playhouse, Chatham, Connecticut."

Zack gave the hotel one last look.

Buh-bye, Mad Dog. See ya! Wouldn't want to be ya.

As soon as they pulled out of the hotel parking lot, Zack heard a strange sizzling sound.

He turned around. Saw a fountain of electrical fireworks shooting out the top of the Marriott sign.

"Wow," said Judy, glancing up at the rearview mirror. "A lightbulb must've blown out. A big one!"

"Yeah," said Zack.

Either that, or Old Sparky wanted to say "buh-bye," too.

The withered 105-year-old man sat slumped in his wheelchair near the cell door.

His ankles were shackled together. A heavy chain drooped in a loop between the rolling chair's footrests. A turban, fashioned from a faded violet bath towel, was wrapped around his skull.

The shriveled old man spoke in a scratchy whisper: "It is time, Hakeem."

"Yes, Professor."

"Take this." He produced a tiny key. "It will open the final compartment. See to it that the anointed one has all that he requires."

"As you command, Exalted One. The boat left Tunisia three weeks ago and arrived safely. The truck from the harbor will arrive tomorrow."

"And the other necessary arrangements?"

"Nearing completion, master."

"Excellent. Well done, Hakeem."

"Thank you, Exalted One."

The professor reached into the tattered pocket of his frayed robe and removed a small slip of paper.

"More names I would add."

Hakeem glanced at the list. "Who is this Mad Dog Murphy you have placed at the top?"

"One who should prove most useful to our cause."

Hakeem tucked the paper away. "Your will shall be done."

"Do not despair, my friend. We two shall meet again. Soon."

Now Habib stepped forward. "When?" he asked. "When are you two meeting again?"

The old man narrowed his milky eyes. "Hakeem, who is this person?"

"His name is Habib, Excellency. He is newly arrived. From Tunis."

"Is he one of us?"

"Of course."

The old man grunted.

"I cannot begin to tell you what an honor it is to finally meet you, sir!" Habib prattled. "I am grievously saddened to hear of your impending death."

The old man gestured with a gnarled claw. "Please. Come closer, Habib. This solitary candle casts but a dim and wavering light. I desire to see your face more fully."

Habib stepped closer to the wheelchair.

"Is this better, Exalted One?"

"Oh, yes. Much."

The withered old man reached up into the cuff of his bathrobe and extracted the bone-handled magician's knife he kept hidden there at all times—a weapon Hakeem had easily smuggled into the prison one day when the ancient guard had been on duty.

"What's that?" asked Habib.

"An omen of *your* impending death."

Hakeem watched in awe as the professor—still possessing the fierce strength of a man eight decades his junior—lurched forward and, with a grunt, jammed the knife blade into Habib's stomach. He twisted it sharply to the right.

Habib crumpled to the floor.

The inmates in the other cells hooted and cheered. Hakeem knew guards would soon be racing up the stairs to investigate the commotion.

The shackled old man rattled chains as he kicked at the limp body.

"Imbecile! Bring me no more such as this one, Hakeem, or next time, I swear by all that is sacred, my blade will find its resting place in your belly!"

Hakeem bowed. "Yes, master."

"We two shall speak again. Soon. When the August moon grows full."

"Yes, master."

"Go. It is time."

And suddenly, the old man's head flopped forward as he rattled out his final breath.

"Master?"

There was no reply.

Hakeem grabbed the knife and slipped out of the cell before any guards arrived.

He knew the professor had died happy with much to look forward to.

Zack, Judy, and Zipper were flying across the state of Connecticut.

Actually, they were on the interstate in Judy's Saab—a type of car built by Swedish guys who also designed jets. North Chester was located in the northwest corner of Connecticut, while Chatham and the theater were over on the east coast—down where the Connecticut River emptied into the Atlantic Ocean. It would take them about two hours to drive across the state.

Judy had a stainless steel tumbler of black coffee in one cup holder and a thermos bottle full of it in the other.

Zipper had the backseat all to himself and was fast asleep.

Zack, riding shotgun, was happy to be leaving Mad Dog, Doll Face, and Old Sparky behind for their Extremely Extended Stay at the Marriott. He didn't think the ghosts would bother his dad. They usually left nonbelievers alone, picked on people like Zack instead.

He let his mind wander.

He imagined the Saab was a real jet.

No, a rocket ship. An intergalactic space cruiser. Cool—
because the inky night sky sparkled with stars.

"There's our destination," Zack thought. *"Third star
on the left! Blast off!"*

"Aye, aye, Cap'n."

He fingered what others might call the window button
but what he knew to be the toggle switch to initiate the
launch sequence. The window opened a half inch. Zack
heard the air whoosh, whine, and whistle. Yep. The rockets were fully operational.

He eyed Commander Judy's control console.

The digital readout behind her circular yoke (which
looked sort of like a steering wheel) glowed with a
green 65.

Judy certainly knew how to pilot a rocket ship: sixty-
five times the speed of light! Incredible. They'd zip past the
moon in about a minute. Faster if nobody needed a bathroom break.

Now Zack observed an obstacle—dead ahead.

"Houston, we have a problem," he thought.

"This is Houston." He imagined a different voice to
keep the dialogue rolling in his head. *"We see it. Appears
to have eighteen rotating drive mechanisms. What in blazes
is it, man?"*

"Some sort of cargo vessel," navigator Zack shot back.
*"The markings on its tail fin flaps suggest it's an inter-
galactic grocery hauler from the planet Krogerus. However, I suspect it's actually a pirate ship carrying concealed
contraband from the mining colony on Melkior Six."*

Judy flicked on her turn signal and, increasing speed, eased into the passing lane.

"*Houston, we are initiating aggressive countermeasures.*"

"*Careful, man!*"

"*Careful? Ha! I laugh in your general direction. Ha, ha, ha!*"

"*You might run into a meteor shower,*" said the nervous radio voice back on earth.

"*No thanks,*" the cocky space cadet voice snapped back. "*I already washed my hair.*"

Zack knew every good space movie needed a couple corny jokes. They called it witty banter.

Suddenly, a glowing missile came flying out of the truck.

A cigarette butt.

Its tip flared red as it left the driver's window and flew like a hot coal shot from a cannon. It would've scored a direct hit on their windshield, but the small car's sleek aerodynamic design sent it up and over the roof!

Ha!

The invisible force field had once again proven to be an excellent defense against sneak butt attacks!

Zack checked out the side-view mirror and saw the cigarette smack into the pavement, where it exploded into a shower of a thousand tiny sparks.

Cigarettes.

They were always out to get him.

Cigarettes were what killed his real mother. Gave her cancer. Of course, she said she only smoked so much because Zack drove her crazy and ruined her life just by being born.

He felt the turbocharger kick in as they eased past the rumbling truck. Zack looked up to give the trucker a wave—just to let the guy behind the wheel know how *not* afraid of flying butts he was.

Only the truck driver wasn't a guy.

It was a woman, a fresh cigarette already jammed between her lips.

She flicked her lighter and Zack saw her face, illuminated by the candling flame.

She looked angry. Furious at the whole world. She looked exactly like his real mother had looked right before she'd gotten sick and died.

Reginald Grimes lurked in the shadows at the back of the auditorium, watching the cast of *Bats in Her Belfry* take their curtain calls.

Near one of the exit alcoves, Grimes noticed a terrified usher. She was staring at him.

So Grimes *glared* at her.

She scurried away.

They always did.

The audience was on its feet now, giving Grimes's staging of the beloved Broadway musical comedy a standing ovation. As the show's director, Grimes did not attend every performance after opening night. But tomorrow he was scheduled to begin rehearsals for *Curiosity Cat*. A perfectionist, Grimes wanted to make certain *Bats* was in the best shape possible before he moved on to his next project.

It was not.

He would need to go backstage. Have a word with the cast.

Heads would roll. Well, at least one very pretty head.

As the audience continued to applaud and thunder "Bravo!," Thurston Powell, the actor playing Dracula, came to center stage to twirl his cape and take his solo bow.

Grimes wondered once again how that must feel.

To savor the limelight. To bask in the glory of a triumphant performance. To soak up the love and adulation of a thousand total strangers.

Yes, there had been a time when Reginald Grimes had dreamed of being a world-renowned actor, but his physical deformity prevented it from ever becoming a reality. As a small child, barely two, he had been left alone in the orphanage laundry with a gas-powered wringer washer. He had, or so he had always been told by the nurse who witnessed the mangling of his left arm, been mesmerized by the machine's rolling cylinders, engineered to squeeze the wash water out of soaked bedsheets. Little Reggie placed his fingertips into the rollers and the ravenous machine had done its job: it had pulled him forward like a limp rag, mashing and crushing his arm up to the elbow.

Forty years and several crude surgeries later, his left arm remained bent and locked at a severe angle. It looked as if it were frozen inside a permanent plaster cast without the need of a sling. Ever since he was a child, fearing the taunts of his classmates, Grimes had worn long-sleeved shirts and sweaters, even in the summer, hoping to forever hide the patchwork of quilted flesh grafted to his ruined arm.

Of course there was no way he could act in Shakespearean tragedies or Broadway comedies without the ability to move his left arm. No way could he become a movie star when the bare skin of his forearm resembled a mound of white cheese slices melted on top of each other.

"Bravo!"

The whole cast was onstage, standing in a line. They locked hands and took one last group bow. When they rose out of it, they beamed.

Grimes grinned.

He knew that at least one of those bright, shiny faces would soon be filled with tears.

10

"Excuse me. Pardon me."

Grimes pushed his way through the standing-room-only crowd to the curtained exit closest to the stage. The house was, of course, packed. The show, completely sold out. Reginald Grimes musicals always were, long before they opened. He had been the Hanging Hill's artistic director for nearly twenty years. Fresh out of drama school (which he had only been able to attend thanks to a scholarship provided by an anonymous donor), he was awarded a generous grant (given by another anonymous donor), to become artistic director of the Pandemonium Players—the acting company in residence at the Hanging Hill Playhouse throughout its repertory season.

He pulled open a door labeled "To Stage," and headed up the cinder block hallway toward the greenroom, the lounge where the cast typically assembled following a performance to meet and greet their friends and adoring fans.

"Good evening, Mr. Grimes!" said the stage manager. "Wasn't the show terrific tonight?"

He narrowed his eyes. "No. It was not. Tell the cast I wish to speak to them. Now."

"Yes, sir."

"Lock the door. No one is to be allowed into this room until I am finished giving my notes."

"Yes, sir!"

As the stage manager assembled all the actors, Grimes stood silently in a dark corner, hidden in the shadows behind a funnel of dusty light cascading down from a dim ceiling fixture. Dressed in a black turtleneck and black slacks, he all but disappeared, although there was no mistaking the sheen from his gleaming coal black eyes. He stroked his pencil-thin mustache. Smoothed his eyebrows with the middle finger of his one good hand.

He waited.

Soon the entire company was standing in a hushed half circle in front of him: Thurston Powell in cape and fangs; Amy Jo and Laura Joy Tiedeman, the actresses playing the tap-dancing Transylvania Twins; the chorus boys and chorus girls decked out in their werewolf and bat costumes.

Grimes didn't say a word. Not at first. He let his stillness fill the terrified thespians with dread. An actor's life was a hard one. Paying jobs were few and far between and it was the director who determined which actors worked and which went back to the unemployment line. Grimes had the power to crush each and every one of their dreams as surely as that horribly antique wringer washer had crushed his.

Finally, he spoke.

"I saw the show tonight." He let his words hang like icicles in the air. "I have a few notes."

Thurston Powell, the dashing leading man, nodded eagerly, pretending to be delighted to hear an honest critique of his performance. The man was a complete suckup. No wonder he played such a convincing vampire.

"Kelly?" said Grimes.

A nervous young showgirl in black tights and sparkling bat wings stepped forward half an inch. The beautiful and talented Kelly Fagan was trembling so much her sequins were shimmering. Her frightened little toes *tappity-tap-tap*ped against the hard tile floor.

Well, well, well.

Hadn't it been just last weekend that this same young woman had refused Reginald Grimes's invitation to dinner? Oh, yes, she had smiled when, quite politely, she said, "I'm already dating someone," but Grimes was certain he had registered the slightest hint of revulsion crossing her pretty face as she contemplated the prospect of being seen in public with a gimp.

Fine. Tonight he would extend her another invitation: to kindly go home.

"You were late for your entrance, Miss Fagan."

"I know," she said, her voice a frightened bird twitter. "We had some trouble making the costume change."

"You were late."

"Right. The bat wings wouldn't . . ."

"You. Were. Late."

"I just missed my entrance by a beat or two . . ."

"No, Ms. Fagan. You missed it by a full measure. Four counts." He tapped his right hand against his stiff left arm. "Five, six, seven, eight! You see, Ms. Fagan, unlike some members of my cast, I pay very strict attention to the conductor waving his baton up and down in the orchestra pit."

"But, I . . ."

"You're fired."

"What?"

"Your services are no longer required. I am terminating your contract, effective immediately."

"But . . ."

He turned to the others in the cast. "Let this be a warning to you all. I will not tolerate unprofessional behavior!"

"But . . . my parents," Fagan sniffled, "my parents were in the audience tonight."

"Really?" said Grimes. "How nice. They were able to see your final performance at the Hanging Hill Playhouse!"

feeling better than he had in weeks, Grimes climbed a winding staircase to the second floor and entered his office.

There was a swarthy man waiting for him.

"Mr. Grimes?"

"Yes?"

"Mr. Reginald Grimes?"

"Yes."

"The orphan child?"

Grimes's pale skin blanched even whiter. "Who. Are. You?"

"My name is Hakeem. We have much to discuss."

11

It was eleven p.m. when Zack, Judy, and Zipper finally pulled off the interstate at the exit for Chatham and the Hanging Hill Playhouse.

The theater was listed on the reflective green sign! Zack was impressed. That meant it was famous. A landmark.

"You know why they call it the Hanging Hill Playhouse?" Judy asked as the Saab eased down the ramp.

Zack had no idea, so he made one up: "Um, it's on top of a hill that sort of hangs out over the river?"

Judy laughed. "No. It used to be a tavern. A place for weary travelers to eat and drink and sleep. A man named Justus Willowmeier built the original Hanging Hill Publick House back in 1854. It was a combination bar, restaurant, hotel, and all-purpose gathering place."

"Have you been talking to Mrs. Emerson again?"

"Yep," said Judy. "She knows everything. She even knows what she doesn't know. The unknown, she looks up."

Mrs. Jeanette Emerson was the librarian back in North Chester and one of Judy's best friends. The two of them could talk about anything and nothing for hours.

They reached a main boulevard and Judy guided the

car into the right-hand lane. Zipper, sensing that they must be getting close to wherever they were going, sprang up in the backseat and leaned his front paws against the window ledge to check out the scenery. Well, it was too dark to see much. So he mostly sniffed.

"We should be able to catch *Bats in Her Belfry* sometime this week. That's the show they're doing on the main stage while we rehearse. It was originally staged at the Hanging Hill, then moved down to New York, where it was extremely successful on Broadway back in 1955. Made Kathleen Williams a star. She sang 'Bitten and Smitten.' Became a top ten hit."

"Cool."

Judy started to hum.

Then sing.

"I'm bitten and smitten and falling in love. He's flittin' and flappin' so high up above. . . ."

"That was a hit?"

"Yeah."

Zack figured they'd never sing it on *American Idol*.

Now they moved through the small-town streets of Chatham, following directional signs for the "World-Famous Hanging Hill Playhouse." At this hour, most of Chatham's shops and restaurants were closed. Cast-iron streetlamps lined the empty sidewalks.

"Wow," said Judy. "What time is it?"

Zack checked his watch. "A little after eleven."

"Guess we got a pretty late start."

"Yeah."

"I hope Mr. Grimes is still at the theater. Zack?"

"Yeah?"

"Mr. Grimes, the director, he has a, well, a reputation."

"Good one?"

"For staging brilliant productions, yes. But as a person, well, they say he can be difficult. Rules the theater with an iron fist."

"Does he make actors cry?"

"Sometimes."

"What about authors?"

"Maybe. I hope not. Anyway, he's the best director for the show. Everybody says so."

"Then," said Zack, "I'll cut him some slack. Won't whip out *my* iron fist unless I have to."

Judy smiled. "Thanks, hon."

"No problem-o." Now it was Zack's turn to say it: "Wow!"

They had just rounded a bend and could see an all-white building glowing atop a hill high on the horizon. Floodlights aimed up toward the ornate molding illuminated the whole front of the five-story-tall mansard root mansion. Only a few windows were lit: one on either side of the fifth floor, one in the middle of the third, and a whole string along the first. The glowing windows gave the Hanging Hill Playhouse two eerily empty eyes, a creepy nose, and a straight-line scowl of square teeth, turning it into a gigantic jack-o'-lantern.

Cars were streaming out of the gravel parking lots on both sides of the building.

"Guess the show just let out," said Judy, maneuvering the car upstream against the tide of theatergoers headed home. They parked in a small lot facing the front porch.

"Let's leave the suitcases in the trunk until we find our rooms."

Since the building used to be a hotel, Zack and Judy would be staying in bedrooms on the upper floors until the show opened.

"Do you know which rooms are ours?" Zack asked.

"Nope. Somewhere up top, I hope."

Zack studied the towers and turrets jutting up from the roof, the clustered stacks of chimneys.

"Cool," he said. "Is there an elevator?"

"I hope so," said Judy.

"What about Zipper? Should we bring him in?"

Zipper, who had been so excited five minutes earlier, was napping again in the backseat. He seemed to be having a dream that involved chasing squirrels: Every so often, his hind legs twitched and kicked.

"Let him sleep," said Judy. "But make sure to leave your window open a crack."

"Roger," said Zack, toggling the rocket switch again. Then he and Judy climbed the porch steps and went into the Hanging Hill Playhouse.

12

His soul swirls in the churning ectoplasm where it has spun in a spiral of overlapping circles for longer than he dares to remember.

He had been roasting in this eternal damnation when he first heard a voice calling him.

"Come forth, Michael Butler, I command you! Diamond Mike, come forth!"

And so he did—carrying his bloody meat cleaver.

He felt his soul chill, then rush up through a swirling current as if trapped under the earth's crust inside a raging geyser. His spirit raced up from the underworld to the brink of life, never quite bursting free or crossing the threshold to the other side of death, never quite coming back to life.

Still, he recalls floating for brief moments across a vast expanse of darkness.

He remembers being hit with blindingly bright lights.

He remembers voices. Screams. Hushed murmurs. Angry men. Terrified women. The sparkle of jewels. Panic.

An audience.

Yes. He had been called into a theater, his summoned spirit put on momentary public display, his movements and very presence orchestrated by a coal-eyed man in a purple turban.

He remembers the turban.

The luminous green jewel shaped like a cockroach sitting at its center.

And then he remembers the man casting him away, sending him back into this numbing limbo to wait until he was called forth once more.

At every appearance, no matter how brief, Diamond Mike Butler longed to be restored to full existence. To be back in his living, breathing body. To rob and steal and kill again.

One time, he nearly made it all the way back.

One time, he almost crossed the threshold.

One time.

Perhaps he will get another chance.

Until then, the demon known in life as Diamond Mike Butler, the Butcher Thief of Bleecker Street, will wait.

He will wait in the churning nothingness beneath this place he remembers hearing the turbaned man calling the Hanging Hill Playhouse.

He will wait.

13

"Mr. Grimes said he'd meet us in the lobby," said Judy.

The lobby was empty.

"What time?" asked Zack.

"I think I told him seven."

In perfect sync, Judy and Zack both glanced at their wristwatches. Eleven-thirty p.m.

"Oops," said Zack.

"Guess we shouldn't have stopped for gas."

"Or dinner."

"Or ice cream cones," said Judy.

Zack said it again: "Oops."

"Tell you what: We'll take a quick look around. If he's already gone home, we can stay at that Holiday Inn we passed on the way into town."

"Okay."

"You take the auditorium. I'll head upstairs and see if he's in his office."

"Cool."

"We meet back here in five minutes."

"Check."

And they split up.

Judy headed up a staircase with an elaborately carved banister. Zack pulled open a door to what he thought was the auditorium.

Turned out it was another staircase. A sign on the wall said Box 2-B and had an arrow pointing up. Fine. He could check out the whole auditorium from an elevated post in the box seats. He bounded up the steps, pushed through a velvety curtain.

"Hello?" he called out. "Mr. Grimes?"

The auditorium was pitch-dark except for the bright light cast from a bare bulb on top of a pole at center stage.

"Mr. Grimes?"

No answer. Just his own voice echoing from the darkness. Zack shrugged and headed for the curtained alcove to take the stairs back down to the lobby.

"Thank you! Thank you all!" a lilting voice called out.

Okay. Mr. Grimes wasn't here, but somebody else sure was.

"Bless you, darlings! Bless you all!"

Zack turned around and made his way back to the edge of the box so he could look down at the shadowy sea of seats. Nothing. Nobody.

"You were a marvelous audience! Marvelous!"

Now he looked toward the stage. The single bulb blinded him a bit, but his eyes soon adjusted.

There, at the lip of the stage, in the shadowy darkness just above the first row of seats, he saw a very grand woman in a jeweled headdress and a ruffled gown. Her crinkly gloves reached up past her elbows. She clutched a bouquet of plump roses and kept bowing and bowing, over and over again.

"Thank you! Bless you! You're too, too kind."

Zack knew the elegant woman had to be a ghost. Nobody had dressed like that since maybe World War I.

"Come back again, my darlings!" she called out to the invisible crowd giving her what must have been the world's first silent ovation. "I'm here for three more weeks!"

Great.

Zack and Judy would be here for three weeks, too.

Zack raced down the steps to the lobby.

Now he had *another* ghost not to tell Judy about. How could he? She had a script to worry about plus a mean director to deal with. She did not need to know about an old-fashioned actress in a jeweled cap who somebody needed to haul offstage with a hook—like they did sometimes in Bugs Bunny cartoons—so they could remind her she was dead!

Judy was waiting for Zack underneath one of the lobby's crystal chandeliers as he slammed the door to the box seats.

"Everything okay?" she asked.

"Yeah," said Zack, a little short of breath after scampering down the staircase. "I just thought I'd, you know, get a little exercise. We've been cooped up in that car for a couple hours. Needed to stretch my legs."

"So you ran down a staircase?"

"Yeah," Zack panted. "Ran up it, too."

"Well, I *walked* up to the second floor. Mr. Grimes wasn't in his office."

"He wasn't in the auditorium, either."

"Guess he got tired of waiting for us."

"Yeah."

"We'd better hit that Holiday Inn."

"Can Zipper stay with us?" asked Zack. "In a hotel?"

"I think so. A lot of hotels are pet-friendly these days. If this one isn't—"

Suddenly, the chandelier over their heads went dark. So did the lights lining the walls. Then the lights in the box office. Zack and Judy were being systematically plunged into darkness, which made the vast expanse of the lobby, with its columns and arched ceilings, as creepy as an empty tomb at midnight.

"Closin' up," called a gruff voice from off in the distance. Zack heard another circuit breaker being thumped off.

"Hello?" Judy called out.

"Closin' up," came the reply from a man they couldn't see.

"Uh, okay. I'm Judy Jennings."

"Aya," said the voice. "We're closin' up."

"Judy *Magruder* Jennings."

"Aya." More switches were flipped with a spring-loaded *flick-click, flick-click.*

"I wrote *Curiosity Cat*?"

"Do tell," said the man, a silhouette moving through the gloom toward them. He was tall and lanky and wore a floppy billed cap that reminded Zack of the hats his toy Confederate army soldiers wore.

"We were supposed to meet Mr. Grimes," said Judy.

"Mr. Grimes is gone," said the shadow.

"I see. Do you work here?"

"Aya."

"I wonder, could you show us to our rooms?"

Now the man stepped into a shaft of soft moonlight streaming through the windows. He was gaunt and grizzled, his cheeks stubbled with the kind of patchy white beard you see on grandfathers who'd forgotten to shave.

He eyeballed them hard. "What rooms?"

"My son and I. We're staying here."

"You can't do that."

"Um, I think we can. It's in my contract. The theater is supposed to provide housing until opening night," said Judy. "They gave us rooms. Upstairs."

"Don't know nothin' about any rooms. Then again, I'm just the janitor."

The janitor. Zack wondered if that was why the man looked so worn out. His face sagged; his baggy eyes drooped; and his lips were frozen in a frown. He appeared to be at least seventy years old and totally tired of mopping floors.

"Okay," said Judy. "We'll come back tomorrow."

The janitor narrowed his eyes. Glared at Zack. "No children are allowed in this theater."

"What?" said Judy.

"No children allowed."

Judy laughed. "I think that's impossible."

"No children!"

"Sir, *Curiosity Cat* is a family show. Families have children."

"Shouldn't."

"What?"

"Shouldn't bring children into this theater. Children bring nothing but trouble."

"Well, I'm sorry you feel that way."

Zack figured the janitor hated kids because they stuck wads of gum and boogers under their seats and he was the one who, months later, had to scrape it all off with a putty knife.

"Well," said Zack, "we'd better hit the road."

"But we'll be back tomorrow," said Judy, sounding a little ticked off. "And we *will* be staying in rooms upstairs. We will also be putting on a show that will bring thousands of children into this theater! Whole busloads of 'em!"

The janitor moved forward. "You don't want to be doin' that."

"Really? Well, just watch me!"

Judy Magruder Jennings never liked it when anybody tried to tell her what she could or could not do. In fact, it was her number one pet peeve.

"Come on, Zack." Yep. She sounded peeved.

Zipper was sitting in the front seat, paws on the steering wheel.

When Zack and Judy opened their doors, he hopped into the back, tail wagging, ready to roll.

"I cannot believe that man!" said Judy, staring back at the dark building.

"Our school janitor hates kids, too," said Zack. "They probably have to list it on their job applications."

Judy laughed.

"Don't worry about it," said Zack. "I'll stay out of his way."

"I guess you're right," said Judy. "Let's go on with the show!"

"Is that another show tune?"

Judy nodded. "From *Annie Get Your Gun*. I guess that janitor really isn't a show person."

Zack played along. "Why's that?"

"They're supposed to smile when they are low."

As they drove away from the theater, Zack glanced at the side-view mirror for one last look at the darkened Hanging Hill Playhouse, perched behind them on the riverbank. Now all the windows were black, so it didn't look like a ginormous jack-o'-lantern anymore, just a deserted haunted house lit by a spooky moon.

Suddenly, Zack saw a flurry of bright flashes flare from casement windows in the basement. It looked like somebody was down there working with a welder's torch.

Or plugging in an electric chair.

The spinning saw blade kept grinding against the rusty lock, sending up a shower of red-hot sparks.

Reginald Grimes and the man who called himself Hakeem were in one of the rooms in the maze that was the basement of the Hanging Hill Playhouse. Sparks streamed off the whirling teeth of the miniature power saw as it gnawed its way though the hinged shackle and lit up the cobweb-coated casement windows behind them.

For whatever reason, Hakeem was attempting to open an ancient steamer trunk that had been triple-looped with heavy chains, the links secured with padlocks.

"How did you know this trunk would be here?" asked Grimes.

Hakeem shut off his power tool and grinned. "Why do you think you are here?"

"What?"

"You were placed here to be the guardian of this treasure chest."

"No. I came here after college to direct plays. Musicals. I am Reginald Grimes!"

"We know this, for we are the anonymous donors who agreed to endow the theater with one million dollars, provided, of course, they hired you to be the company's artistic director."

"Nonsense."

"We are the same benefactors who made certain you received a college degree in either theater or theology."

Grimes was shocked.

Theater or theology.

That was precisely what his guidance counselor at the High School for Orphans and Helpless Youth had told him: An anonymous donor was willing to pay for his room, board, and college tuition, provided he studied theology or theater. At the time, Grimes had thought the bequest rather peculiar if not downright ridiculous. Why two subjects so alphabetically linked? Why the fixation on "t-h-e" degrees? He would have been foolish, of course, to turn down the offer for reasons related to spelling, because it was his ticket out of the orphanage, a chance to show the world the special talents he knew he had.

Grimes chose theater because he felt studying theology would have been a complete waste of his time, since he had stopped believing in God long ago—at least, any benevolent, all-powerful, halfway-caring god.

Hakeem's saw blade started whirring again, chewing through the final lock's steel shackle. Grimes shielded his eyes from the spew of sparks.

"Why me?" he called out over the harsh whine of steel on steel.

The final lock popped free. Hakeem turned off his power tool.

"I knew your grandfather."

"Impossible. I have no family."

"So you have always been told. However, in truth, you are the sole surviving male heir of a very noble line. Your family tree has its roots in antiquity and the most glorious civilization to ever spring forth along the coasts of the Mediterranean Sea!"

"Nonsense. I was raised in an orphanage."

"For your own protection."

"What?"

"We placed you there."

"You put me in that godforsaken pit on purpose?"

"It was for the best."

"Really? The best?" Rage engorged Grimes's soul. His mangled left arm twitched at the shoulder. "Who do you think you are?"

"I am your loyal and obedient servant, Royal High Priest."

"What?"

"I live only to serve and protect the true descendants of the high priest of Ba'al Hammon, lord of the incense altar, chief god of Carthage, consort of the goddess Tanit."

"You're a religious fanatic! No wonder you wanted me to study theology. But why theater?"

"Much religious ritual requires a certain theatricality," said Hakeem. "We desired that you would receive the training required to stage our most spectacular rites."

"Who are you people? Who is this 'we' you keep talking about?"

"The Brotherhood of Hannibal. Those who live but to see Carthage rise to its former glory!"

"Hannibal? The warrior who marched elephants over the Alps to attack ancient Rome?"

"The same, Exalted One."

Hakeem bowed, his hands clasped together in a tent of supplication.

Grimes liked the bowing bit. Liked being called Exalted One, too. Maybe he could forgive his "loyal servants" for dumping him in a home for unwanted children if they all treated him this way.

"So," he said, "you knew my grandfather?"

"Indeed, sire. He was a remarkably talented man."

"What about my father? My mother?"

"I knew of them."

"Are they alive?"

Hakeem shook his head. "Sadly, they are both deceased. You are the sole surviving male heir. You are the one chosen to fulfill the prophecy."

Now Grimes felt his chest swell with pride.

The chosen one.

"Very well," he said, assuming the bearing of a haughty high priest. "What, pray tell, is inside this dusty trunk?"

"Much."

"Open it!" Grimes commanded.

"As you say, Exalted One." Hakeem pried apart the lid.

Grimes smelled mothballs. On one side, he saw dark costumes hanging on a closet rod; on the other, a stack of drawers, each with its own brass pull. The top drawer had a keyhole.

"We will open this locked compartment in due time," said Hakeem.

"You have the key?"

"Yes."

"Then open it now!" Grimes demanded.

"First you must read this." Hakeem pulled open the second drawer and extracted a book the size of a big-city phone directory. The leather cover was crackled with age.

"What's in this book?" asked Grimes as he felt the ancient volume's heft.

"Your destiny!"

After spending the night at the Holiday Inn, Zack, Judy, and Zipper drove back to the Hanging Hill Playhouse first thing Sunday morning.

Zack liked the Holiday Inn. They stayed in one of the nonhaunted rooms. The only things sizzling in the breakfast room were the microwaved sausage links.

"The table meeting is at ten a.m.," said Judy.

Zipper whined quizzically.

"You're meeting a table?" asked Zack.

"That's what they call it when the director, designers, writer, composer, and cast all get together for the first time. You sit around a big table, everybody introduces themselves, and then the actors read the script out loud."

"Cool," said Zack. "Can I come?"

"Sure."

They parked in the spot where they had parked the night before. Zack looked up at the big white building perched on its hump of a hill. In the bright morning sunshine, it looked like a wedding cake with lots of frosting ribbons rippled around the edges.

A woman came out to the porch and started waving at them.

"That's Monica," said Judy. "She's the company manager."

"Welcome to the Hanging Hill!" the young woman called out with an enthusiasm bubbly enough to rival Judy's. "We're so glad you made it! Was the drive okay?"

"Fine," said Judy. "This is my stepson, Zack."

"The one the script's dedicated to?"

"The same," said Judy. "We arrived late last night."

"Really?"

"Very late," Judy said with a smile. "The janitor kicked us out."

"Oh, don't mind him. That's Wilbur Kimble. He's been here so long he thinks he runs the place. Come on, I'll show you to your rooms."

Zipper barked.

"Uh," said Zack, "I think Zipper may need to see the bathroom first. I'll take him around back for quick walk."

"Good idea," said Judy. "I'll go inside with Monica, grab our room keys, and meet you guys in the lobby."

"Cool. Come on, Zip."

Zack and Zipper strolled up a shaded sidewalk paralleling the Connecticut River behind the theater for a couple hundred yards.

While Zipper sniffed, found the perfect patch of grass,

and did his business, Zack glanced back at the theater. The basement windows were dark this morning. No sparks popping like flashes from a digital camera on hyperdrive. Maybe Mad Dog Murphy hadn't followed him here after all.

"Come on, Zip," Zack said when they reached the end of the river walk. "We better head back!"

Zipper wagged his tail and led the way.

Zack watched a long black limousine pull into the parking lot behind the theater near a loading dock for trucks hauling scenery. In fact, a big eighteen-wheeler was parked there now.

The limousine, on the other hand, was probably hauling one of the famous actors arriving for Judy's first meeting with the cast. Zack hoped it was Tomasino Carrozza, the hysterically funny clown who would be playing the title character, Curiosity Cat. When he was little, Zack had seen Carrozza do some incredibly hilarious stuff as a regular on *Sesame Street*.

"Come on, Zip! I want to get Carrozza's autograph!"

They scooted down the path into the parking lot just as a chauffeur marched around the stretch limousine to pull open the rear door.

A kid stepped out. A blond boy, about Zack's age. Wearing a navy blue blazer, khaki pants, and some sort of silk scarf tucked into the collar of his shirt.

As soon as the boy saw Zack and Zipper, he started to wheeze.

And sneeze.

70

A blond woman with a drum-tight face stepped out of the limo. She had an orangish, Oompa-Loompa tan.

"Remove your dog immediately," she snapped at Zack. "Or I will be forced to summon security!"

"I'm allergic," whined the boy. He started to gasp and rattle while his mother did karate chops across his back. "I wanna go home!"

"We can't go home, honey!" She karate-chopped harder. "We signed a contract, remember?"

"B-b-but this is a musical, Mommy! I c-c-can't sing!" His words stuttered out as his mother's fists flamenco-danced up and down his spine.

"You're a star, Derek! A Hollywood star!"

"Yes, Mommy."

Zack finally realized the hyperventilating blond boy was Derek Stone, former star of the *Ring My Bell* sitcom on ABC. His dimpled cheeks and boyish grin had been on the cover of about a billion magazines, because nine-year-old girls everywhere thought he was "Hot!" Or at least that was what they thought until he hit ten and got fired from the show, and some other blond with dimples took over his part.

"Young man? The dog?" Mrs. Stone flicked her hand to shoo Zack and Zipper away. Bracelets clacked.

"Sorry," said Zack. When he bent down to scoop up Zipper, he heard a bicycle skid to a stop.

"Hey, Derek." It was a girl, also about Zack's age. "You're not afraid of a little mutt like that, are you?"

Derek struck a hand-on-hip pose and looked like he

might be modeling underwear for a Sears catalog. "Afraid? Don't be ridiculous, Meghan."

The girl on the bike thrust out her hand toward Zack. "Hey. I'm Meghan McKenna."

Wow. Meghan McKenna. *The* Meghan McKenna.

"Uh, hi. I'm Zack. Zack Jennings."

"Cool. Any relation to Judy Magruder Jennings?"

"She's my mom. Well, my stepmom. But she's not mean or anything like all the wicked stepmothers in the fairy tales and stuff."

"Well, she's an awesome author!" said Meghan. "*Curiosity Cat Spies a Pigeon* was the first book I ever read and I totally *love* everything she's written since!"

"So do we!" gushed Mrs. Stone. "We've enjoyed her entire oeuvre!"

Zack had no idea what an "oeuvre" was. It sounded like "oov-rah." Maybe it was a vacuum cleaner. Or a body part near your nose.

"She means they've read everything your stepmom ever wrote," Meghan explained.

"Oh. Thanks," Zack said to Mrs. Stone. "Did you like *Curiosity Cat Bakes a Cake*?"

"Marvelous! Incredible! Her best book ever!"

Zack grinned. So did Meghan. They both knew there was no such book.

"Well," said Zack, "I need to go inside and unpack before the table meeting."

"Are you in the show?" Meghan asked.

"No. I'm not an actor. You're playing Claire, right?"

"Yeah, and I'm totally psyched! Claire is a great character!"

"Well, I know my stepmom was excited to hear you were available to do the part." Casting Meghan had been what Judy called "a home run." Meghan had already won a Golden Globe and had even been nominated for an Oscar.

Meghan shrugged. "I told my mom I just *had* to do this role. Hey, I'd do it for free!"

Mrs. Stone gave Derek a quick elbow to the ribs.

"I am also thrilled to be here," he said, attempting to sound sincere but not doing a very good job of it.

"Hey, what's your dog's name?" Meghan asked Zack.

"Zipper."

"Neat. Cool name. See you around, Zack!"

When Meghan McKenna flashed Zack her million-dollar movie-star smile, he almost dropped his dog. Zipper barked and panted and wagged his tail.

Apparently, he was a major-league Meghan McKenna fan, too.

Zack and Zipper climbed the loading dock steps.

The wide warehouse door had been rolled down tight, so they went into the theater through a smaller door off to the side. As soon as it slid shut behind them, they were plunged into inky blackness.

"Hello?"

Zack realized he and Zipper were backstage. Faint light glowed up ahead, leaking through the doorways and windows cut into scenery panels.

"Hello?"

He walked toward the light, past long tables covered with brown paper and filled with all sorts of hand props for the Dracula musical. Wooden stakes. Strings of garlic cloves. Jars of fake blood.

"Hello?"

His voice echoed off the stage's towering brick walls.

He put Zipper down. The dog's toenails clicked across the bare floor as he headed downstage toward a door in a wall made out of wooden slats and tightly stretched canvas.

Through that doorway, Zack could see the bare bulb glowing inside its metal cage—the same pole lamp he had seen last night from up in the box seats.

"What are *you* doing here?"

It was the grizzled old janitor. Wilbur Kimble. He came shuffling across the stage, pushing a wobble-wheeled mop bucket.

"Sorry. I guess we came in the wrong door and got lost."

"Bad place to get lost."

Kimble moved closer. In the harsh light of the single naked bulb, Zack could see that unlike the mannequin-faced Mrs. Stone, this guy was creased like a sunbaked mud pie.

"You in the show?" the old man asked.

"No, sir."

"Good."

"Yeah," said Zack, trying to sound friendly. "Because I can't really sing or act. I can dance a little—but not the kind of dancing people would actually pay money to see someone do."

The old man wasn't smiling.

"Beware Pandemonium!" he whispered dramatically.

"Hunh?"

"Beware Pandemonium!"

"Oh-kay. Will do. Thanks."

The old man pointed a gnarled finger toward a red exit sign. "Go! Get out of here before it's too late!"

"Yes, sir!" Zack turned and almost tripped over the thick electrical cable snaking across the floor.

"Careful, boy! You'll pull down the ghost light!"

Zack froze. "The what?"

The old man gestured toward the solitary lamp.

"The ghost light. It burns onstage all night, every night."

Great. A ghost light.

The janitor creaked his rolling bucket forward. "Every theater has one. You know why we call it a ghost light?"

Zack thought fast. "Um, because if you didn't leave it on, people would stumble around in the dark, fall off the stage, crack open their skulls, and turn into ghosts?"

The old man shook his head then peered into the darkness above their heads. "No. We leave it on as a courtesy. To help all the ghosts haunting this theater find the children who shouldn't be here!"

Zack looked up into the dim fly space climbing high above the stage. It was filled with ropes and scenery panels and curtains and darkness.

He couldn't see any floating fiends or phantoms.

But that didn't mean they weren't up there, biding their time, waiting for a chance to swoop down and terrify Zack.

They'd probably all heard how special he was.

18

Zack saw Judy and Monica the Company Manager near the box office, which looked like an elaborately decorated circus wagon with bank-teller windows.

Zipper barked.

"Hey, Zack!" Judy waved them over.

"Sorry we're late. Zip and I ran into some of the actors out back."

"Who?"

"Meghan McKenna!"

"Really?"

"Yeah!"

"Did you get her autograph?"

"Not yet."

Judy was excited. "Well, get one for me when you do!"

The company manager beamed. "We were all so thrilled to hear that Miss McKenna, an actual Oscar nominee, would be joining the Pandemonium Players!"

There was that word again. "Pandemonium?" Zack asked.

"That's what we call our resident acting company," Monica explained.

"Cool," said Zack, wondering why the janitor wanted him to beware of a bunch of actors. They seemed pretty harmless. Unless, of course, that kid Derek sneezed all over you.

Judy handed Zack a brass key. "Monica and I need to get the scripts organized for the table meeting. Why don't you take Zipper up to the room, make sure he has water, and then meet us downstairs in rehearsal room A? We're on the very top floor!"

"Awesome. Oh, I forgot to tell you—I also met Derek Stone."

"Who?"

"You know, the Hollywood guy who used to be on *Ring My Bell*?"

Judy looked confused.

"It's a TV show. He's not on it anymore."

"Oh," said Judy. "I see. He's one of the adults in the cast."

"No. He's a boy. About my age. I guess he's playing Charlie."

"No, Brad Doyle is playing Charlie," said Judy. "He's a Broadway actor from New York."

"Uh," said the company manager, "Derek Stone was a last-minute replacement. Signed him on yesterday."

Now Judy seemed shocked. "Really?"

"Yes. Brad Doyle got sick. Very, very sick."

"Have you memorized your lines, Derek?"

"No. Not completely."

"What's taking you so long?"

"I just got the script yesterday, Mom."

"And?"

Derek Stone hung his head. He and his mother were striding across the carpeted lobby of the Hanging Hill Playhouse, on their way to rehearsal room A for the first read-through and table meeting.

Derek didn't want to be here.

He couldn't sing. In fact, he scared the neighbor's pets when he tried. Yes, driving around in a chauffeured limousine was fun but what he really wanted was to go home to Marina del Rey so he could race his remote control monster truck up and down the driveway some more.

"Chin up," said his mother. "You're a star, Derek. Act like one. Stop slouching."

Derek did as he was told. He held himself erect and moved swiftly. He smiled and nodded at everyone they passed. He even tucked one hand into the side pocket of his blazer while letting his other arm swing freely at his side. He'd seen a British prince walk that way once on TV. It looked suave.

Derek Stone would make his mother happy and try to act like a great actor.

He just wished he really were one.

It would make all the pretending so much easier.

Judy and the company manager headed for the down staircase and rehearsal room A.

Zack and Zipper hurried across the lobby to the elevator. He kept pushing the up button until he finally read the sign hanging on the sliding cage door:

OUT OF SERVICE

That meant he and Zipper would have to climb the steps.

All the way to the fifth floor.

21

Bleary-eyed, Reginald Grimes sat at the desk in his office, devouring the curling pages of the thick book.

"I have a table meeting at ten," he mumbled. "Shouldn't miss it." He kept speed-reading.

He had been up all night with the ancient text and was nearing the end of *The Book of Ba'al,* which was filled with astonishingly incredible spells and incantations, amazingly powerful rituals and rites.

In the first pages of the book, he had found his family tree, something every orphan dreams of one day discovering. He learned that not only did he have a father and a grandfather, he had two thousand years of history and could trace his roots all the way back to Carthage and the supreme high priests of Ba'al Hammon.

He felt as if he were in a hypnotic trance. Maybe it was the lack of sleep or all the coffee he had been guzzling. Grimes remembered the time when the orphanage doctors had attempted to surgically repair his withered arm years after the incident with the wringer washer. They had put him under with ether, an anesthetic that had sent him swimming through a murky pool of sleep and dreams. He felt the same way now, under the spell of this intoxicating book.

"The children have arrived," said Hakeem, standing guard at the office door. Two Tunisian musclemen had accompanied Hakeem to the theater this morning: One was named Badir, the other Jamal.

"Hmmm?"

"The chosen children. They are here. Young Miss McKenna and Master Stone."

Grimes looked up from the book. "Master who?"

"Stone," said Hakeem. "Derek Stone."

"Who in blazes is he?"

"The young boy who will be playing the leading juvenile in your next production."

"Charlie?"

Hakeem nodded.

"Bah! I cast Brad Doyle for that part!"

"Have you not heard? Young Master Doyle has taken ill. It came over him quite suddenly."

Grimes thought he heard one of the burly thugs guarding the door chuckle.

"Besides," Hakeem continued, "Master Stone is better suited for the role. He has—how shall I put this?—the same *qualifications* as Miss McKenna."

"Really? Says who?"

"The financial backers of *Curiosity Cat*."

"Oh. You've spoken to my producers? Because I never have. I am given to understand that they are very wealthy, very busy men."

Hakeem smiled. "Indeed. We are. Very, very busy."

22

Yesterday Zack had thought it was totally awesome that they'd be sleeping in what was basically the Hanging Hill Playhouse's attic. Now, as he and Zipper rounded the landing for the second floor, he wasn't so sure.

"Only three more floors to go," he said. He was panting. Zipper wasn't. Zack hoped that they'd get the elevator fixed before he and Judy had to haul in their luggage. Otherwise, they'd be *lugging* it up five flights of stairs.

Trudging up to the third floor, Zack heard a little girl giggling.

Probably Meghan McKenna, Zack thought. He held on to the handrail. Leaned out. Peered up.

He saw nothing except the space between alternating flights of stairs and the bottoms of the billion metal steps he and Zipper still had left to climb.

"Come on, Zip."

They hiked up to the landing between the second and third floors.

That's where they heard more giggles.

"Meghan?" Zack called out. "Is that you?"

No answer.

"This is pretty funny, hunh? Guess the elevator's so old it croaked."

Another laugh. No. A howl.

This time it came from a man. From below.

"The devil led me on!" A raw voice rang out.

Now Zack heard plodding footsteps.

Someone was climbing up the staircase—behind them!

"The devil led me on!"

"Come on, Zip." Zack picked up his dog and started taking the stairs two at a time. Behind them, the footfalls continued.

Click. Clunk.

Heavy boot heels hitting steel.

Click. Clunk.

Zack's heart was pounding hard. He could feel Zipper's racing, too.

"Don't worry, Zip. I'm here."

Zipper barked and his sharp yap rang like a bell in a tiny tiled bathroom.

The girl upstairs giggled again.

"Meghan?" Zack gasped. "Is that you?" Each word took more air than he had in his lungs. Each breath took more effort than the breath before.

Click. Clunk. Click. Clunk.

"The devil led me on!"

Zack spun around.

Saw nothing. No one.

But he did feel an icy chill pass right through him!

Clack. Clunk.

Clack. Clunk.

Now the footsteps were *in front* of him!

Zack didn't move.

"Beware of that one," whispered a voice.

Slowly, very slowly, Zack tiptoed up to the next landing, where he really, really, really hoped he'd find Meghan McKenna hidden in the shadows, doing a spooky voice.

Only it wasn't Meghan.

It was another girl. Younger. Five, maybe six. She was juggling three balls high above her head. Her skin was ashen. Her dress was ruffled, her hair tied up in a big red bow.

"Beware!" she whispered again. "He's one of the others!" And then she vanished.

Suddenly, at the top of the stairwell, Zack heard a wooden trapdoor swing open. A man screamed.

Zack leaned over the handrail, looked up.

The soles of two hobnailed boots came hurtling straight down at him!

He snapped back and watched the falling man yank to a stop.

Another ghost.

And this one was wearing *really* old clothes. Long boots with buckles, pants buttoned near the knees, and a cloak with a broad white collar. As he dangled in the narrow space between the staircases, Zack realized that this ghost looked exactly like a Thanksgiving Pilgrim without his hat.

Except those Pilgrims didn't usually have nooses around their necks.

23

Reginald Grimes rose from his chair.

"So you people, you brothers of Hannibal, you fancy yourself theatrical producers?"

"Only when it suits our purposes, Exalted One," Hakeem replied humbly.

"Is that so?" Grimes was furious. He balled up his good hand into a fist and banged it hard against his desk. "How dare you change my cast without consulting me first!"

Hakeem bowed slightly. "It was for the best."

"Oh, really? For the best? Explain that to me, Mr. Hakeem."

"In good time, High Priest. In good time."

"Bah! Now!"

Hakeem raised his eyes. Smiled. "First, you must prove yourself worthy of our trust."

Grimes scoffed at that. "What? *You* dare audition *me*?"

"Yes," said Hakeem thoughtfully. "We do."

"I am Reginald Grimes!"

"We know that."

"I audition for no one."

"Really? Not even when the role we offer will give you wealth and power beyond your wildest imaginings?"

That gave Grimes pause.

"How much wealth and power?"

"More than any mortal man has ever known."

Oh. He liked the sound of that. He liked it a lot.

"Very well, gentlemen. For the time being, I accept your cast change. I will work with this new boy. What's his name?"

"Stone. Derek Stone."

"He's right for the part?"

"He and Meghan are both perfect."

Grimes returned to his chair. Leaned back. "I am curious about one thing. Why did your so-called brotherhood choose to produce *Curiosity Cat*? Why not *Bats in Her Belfry*?"

"*Curiosity Cat* provides that which we require. The two children. This sacred power spot. The full August moon. Even now the portal begins to open."

Grimes grimaced and reopened the ancient text sitting atop his desk. He frantically flipped through the pages—forward, then backward—hoping to find some explanation, maybe something he had missed the first time through. *Two children? August moon? Sacred power spots?*

"The answers you seek are not revealed in that text," said Hakeem. "To find them, we must open the secret compartment, to which I alone have the key—the key personally handed to me by your glorious grandfather."

"So let's go open it!"

"No. First you must finish reading all that is written in *The Book of Ba'al* and my men must install the scenic piece that arrived only this morning."

"You're changing my scenery, too?"

"This prop will not appear onstage. However, I am happy to report, it was delivered in most excellent condition, having traveled across the sea from Tunisia."

"Tunisia?" said Grimes. "You people imported scenery we're not even going to use—all the way from Tunisia?"

"Yes," said Hakeem.

"You're insane!"

"Actually, we prefer the term 'devout.'"

"Soon," he hears them say.

"Soon!" It is hissed by a hundred voices slithering around him in the swirling cesspool of disembodied demons and devils beneath the theater, all yearning to live once more.

"Soon the moon grows full!"

"The portal begins to widen."

"The two children have arrived!"

"Soon we shall see the red moon!"

"Soon comes the lightning moon!"

"The dog moon!"

The demon spirits howl and cackle and hiss again in harmony: "Sssooooon!"

Diamond Mike Butler, the Butcher Thief of Bleecker Street, feels hope swell once more in his decay-riddled soul.

Soon the full August moon will rise in the sky. Soon he will rise as well.

And, if all goes as promised, this time he will also cross the precipice to life, where he will once again pillage and plunder and cause more people to die!

25

Wilbur Kimble, who was more than eighty years old, had worked at the Hanging Hill Playhouse all his life, dating back to when it was a stop on the old vaudeville circuit.

He pushed his broom into rehearsal room A and sized up the dozen or so people milling about drinking coffee. Actors. Designers. The stage manger. Kimble recognized Tomasino Carrozza. Talented man. Could've been a headliner back in the days of vaudeville, when you had to have talent or the audience would toss rotten tomatoes at you. Literally. Janitor's job was even harder back then.

Kimble shoved his broom underneath the folding table where the producers had set up a coffee urn, hot cocoa, juice boxes, paper cups, muffins, bagels, and doughnuts.

Cocoa. Juice boxes.

That was because there were kids in this show. A couple of actors from out in Hollywood.

Kids.

Wilbur Kimble hated seeing children in the theater. Made his job that much harder.

He ran his broom along the baseboard so he could move around the room and eyeball the woman who intended to live at the theater for three weeks with her son. Apparently, from what he'd seen on the posters up in the lobby, this Judy Magruder Jennings was a big-deal children's book author.

"Excuse me? Sir?"

Kimble turned. A bottled blonde who appeared to be smuggling soccer balls under her blouse was waving at him. Her bracelets kept clacking against each other.

"Aya?" said Kimble.

"My son spilled his apple juice." She gestured at a boy in a blue blazer. The bratty Little Lord Fauntleroy was holding his juice box upside down and squeezing it like he was milking a cardboard cow, fascinated by not only the squirts but the gassy fart sounds they made. Boy seemed a bit peculiar. Maybe dim-witted, too.

"This apple juice is dangerous!" the boy whined out his nose. "I'm fructose intolerant!"

Some of the adults were staring at the kid, wondering what kind of holy terror they'd be spending the rest of their summer with. Well, the little monster didn't scare Kimble. He'd seen his type before. What they lacked in talent, they made up for with hot air and temper tantrums.

The boy dropped his crumpled juice box to the floor. His mother wiggled her fingers to indicate exactly where Kimble needed to mop up.

Stage mothers. The spoiled brats and crybabies always had one.

"Has anyone seen Miss McKenna?" the stage manager called out.

"Her mother must've let her sleep in," said juice boy's stage mother. "Maybe because Meghan is a 'movie star.'" The blonde made quote marks in the air. Sounded jealous.

"I'm waiting for my son, too," said the playwright.

"We have a few more minutes," said the stage manager. "Reginald is running late."

Kimble pushed his broom out of the room

Kids.

Three of 'em.

Two in the show plus the writer's son.

There hadn't been any children at the Hanging Hill Playhouse since that ill-fated production of *The Music Man,* a show that had been forced to close early because all the children in the cast quit.

They were all too terrified to work at the theater. Seemed they kept seeing ghosts.

Kimble smiled.

Maybe he could convince these three to go home, too.

Zack decided he'd skip the table meeting.

They'd be rehearsing the show for three whole weeks, so what was the big deal about being there for the first read-through?

Why not give the Pilgrim Guy a chance to vacate the premises?

There was a knock on the door.

Ghosts usually didn't knock; they more or less seeped their way in. But maybe this was a trick.

Another knock.

"Zack?"

It was a girl and she sounded older than the juggling ghost.

"It's me. Meghan. Zack? I know you're in there. I can see your feet."

Zack glanced at the door and saw that there was a huge gap between its bottom and the floorboards, because the building was so old it sagged.

"Oh, hi!" he said "I was just getting Zipper some water."

"Cool. Hey, how come you wear two different kinds of socks?"

Zack looked at his feet: one red, one argyle. Another mismatched pair, courtesy of the sock gremlins.

"Um . . ." He tried to think of a good explanation. "Uh." There wasn't one.

"It's a cool look," said Meghan. "I mean, who says socks have to match? Why not wear a different one on each foot? Mind if I steal the idea and start mixing up my socks, too?"

"Uh, no. Sure. Go ahead."

"Thanks. You going down to the table meeting?"

"I dunno," said Zack. "Are you?"

"Uh, yeah. I'm in the show, remember?"

"Oh, yeah. Right."

"You wanna head down with me?"

"You mean together?"

"Uh, yeah."

Moment of truth. Admit that he was still slightly afraid of ghosts, especially any that dive-bombed down stairwells with nooses wrapped around their necks, or leave the room to be with a girl who might turn into a pretty neat new friend?

"Okay," said Zack. He rose from the bed. Patted Zipper on the head. The dog moaned slightly but he was sound asleep, nestled tight against the pillows.

"We'd better hurry. My mom says I shouldn't be late for my first day of work."

"Okay." Zack walked toward the door.

"Oh, by the way, the elevator's still broken. We'll have to take the stairs."

He hesitated. Ran through his options again. Hide under the bed? Hike down the steps with Meghan? He took in a long, deep breath.

"Okay," he said.

27

Meghan and Zack clomped down the stairs.

"Did you know that the hill this theater is built on used to be called Hangman's Hill?"

Zack froze. "What?"

"In the olden days, public hangings were spectacles. People would come from miles around to see a good execution."

"Uuh-hunh."

"This hill was the perfect spot to put on a show because you could see the gallows for about a mile in any direction!"

"Whattaya know." Zack tried to laugh. "Henh-henh-henh."

"You feeling okay?"

"Yeah."

"You don't sound so hot."

"Motel vending machine food for dinner last night. Chili."

"Oh. Come on."

They started descending the steps again.

"Anyway," said Meghan, "my mom's a history buff.

Whenever we're on the road or on location, she researches everything she can about the place we're going to. That's why they call this the Hanging Hill Playhouse. Well, first it was the Hanging Hill Publick House."

"Right," said Zack. That was as far back as Judy's theater history lesson had gone yesterday. She'd never made it all the way back to ye olde scaffold-and-noose days.

"My mom's heading back to the library today to learn more."

Zack thought about asking Meghan's mom if she knew of any Pilgrims who had dangled from the gallows on Hangman's Hill. Maybe they'd hanged juggling girls, too. Zack couldn't figure out why anybody would do that. Mimes, maybe. But not jugglers.

As they marched down the steps, the hard rubber heels of their running shoes thudded against the metal treads. The deep ringing sound reverberated off the stairwell walls.

"Sounds like bells, hunh?" said Meghan.

"Yeah," said Zack. "Church bells."

"I think theaters are a lot like churches," said Meghan.

"Because of all the pageantry and costumes and stuff?"

"That plus the big emotions trapped inside both buildings. In churches, you have the joy of weddings, the sadness of funerals."

"And in a theater," said Zack, "you have comedies and tragedies."

"Exactly. The walls soak it all up. I figure that's why so many churchyards and theaters are haunted."

Zack froze again. This time in midstep. "What?"

"A lot of theaters attract ghosts, Zack. Every playhouse I've ever worked in had at least one."

"Really?"

"Sure. There was this theater where the balcony seats kept folding down all by themselves because a bunch of ghosts wanted to see our show."

"Unh-hunh."

They started walking down the steps again.

"There's this theater in Ohio that's haunted by a wealthy woman whose husband shot her when he found out she had, like, a major crush on the show's leading man. You can still see her up in the balcony, waiting for her handsome hero to make his next entrance, which, of course, he never does, so she just sits there and sighs forlornly."

They clunked down to the second floor.

"Meghan," said Zack tentatively, "do you really believe in ghosts? Do you really see them?"

"Well, duh. Don't you?"

"What about this theater? Is it haunted?"

"Uh, I think so." She pointed down the steps. "That girl down there? Come on. She *has* to be a ghost. Nobody would wear a dress like that unless they were dead."

Zack whipped around just in time to see the little girl disappear.

This time she was juggling bowling pins.

28

This was so cool!

Meghan McKenna was a kindred spirit. A fellow Ghost Seer!

"Not everyone can see them," Zack said as they raced across the lobby and headed for the curving staircase leading down to the rehearsal room.

"I know," said Meghan. "Especially not adults!"

"Yeah. Except at night. Just about *everybody* can see ghosts at night."

"Only if the ghosts *want* to be seen."

"Or if the living person really wants to see the ghost. Like at a séance, or something."

"True," said Meghan. "And even when you can't see 'em, you can usually hear 'em—*if* they want to be heard."

"Exactly!" said Zack.

"You can sort of feel 'em, too," said Meghan. "Wind, chills, goose bumps."

"I know! I felt the Pilgrim walk right through me!"

"What Pilgrim?"

"Oh, he's this guy who hangs himself in the stairwell."

"Neat. Must've been one of the original stars here at the Hanging Hill. Guess he's stuck here."

"Yeah. They keep him on a short leash."

Meghan laughed.

"I think Juggler Girl is afraid of him."

"How come?"

"She said some stuff that made me think she and the Pilgrim weren't playing on the same team."

"Like what?"

Zack did his best Juggler Girl impression: *"Don't listen to that one. He's one of the others. Whooo-oooh!"*

"Wow! What did she mean? One of the others?"

Zack shrugged. "I don't know."

"Well . . . we need to find out."

"We do?"

"Definitely. Aren't you curious?"

"I guess."

"Come on, Zack. Curiosity helps us see just how lively life can be!"

"Hey, that's from *Curiosity Cat!*"

"I know. I sing it in the first act! Best number in the whole show!"

They entered the rehearsal room.

The cast, including a gangly guy with googly eyes and a goofy face—Zack recognized him immediately as Tomasino Carrozza—sat around cafeteria-type tables set up in a horseshoe.

A ghoulish-looking man with a mustache as thin as an

eraser smudge sat in the center of the middle table. Zack figured he must be Reginald Grimes, the world-famous director. A dark-skinned man wearing a red hat that resembled an upside-down sand bucket with a tassel on top sat next to him.

Judy was at the first table to the left. Zack gave her a nervous wave and found a chair in the back of the room, near the coffeepot.

"Sorry I'm late," said Meghan as she hurried to an empty chair at a table full of actors. "The elevator's still broken."

Then nobody said anything.

A few adults coughed or cleared their throats.

Some nibbled on baked goods. Meghan chomped into a doughnut, which was a good thing as far as Zack was concerned. Meant his new friend wasn't a ghost. The spooks he'd met in North Chester never ate anything, not even the chubby ones!

Everybody kept waiting for the director to speak.

Only, the director wasn't speaking. He was sitting at that center table, eyes glued to the pages of some musty old book that wasn't the script to *Curiosity Cat*. It was too thick, the size of the New York City Yellow Pages.

"Sir?" said the company manager.

Nothing.

"Mr. Grimes?"

It seemed as if Mr. Grimes couldn't hear her. It also looked like he hadn't slept in weeks.

"Reginald?"

"Hmmm?"

Finally.

"Everybody's here, sir."

"Hmmm?"

"Everyone's assembled for the table meeting."

Grimes sighed. Seemed perturbed.

He stood up and traced a finger across both eyebrows and his mustache, maybe to make sure they were lined up just the way he liked them. Zack noticed that Mr. Grimes never used his left arm. It looked paralyzed, cocked at a slight angle by his side.

"Welcome to the Hanging Hill Playhouse," the director mumbled quickly. "Hakeem?" Grimes sat down, returned to his book. The even scarier man in the red hat stood up.

"Greetings. I am Hakeem. I will be assisting Mr. Grimes on this, his most glorious production ever."

The actors applauded.

Grimes's eyes remained glued to the big book. He flipped forward a page.

"While our esteemed director studies his production notes," said Hakeem, "let us all read the script out loud."

Grimes slammed the book, sending up a puffy cloud of dust. Derek Stone sneezed.

"Finished!" said Grimes.

"Excellent," said Hakeem. "We are about to read out loud from the script."

"Read?" said Grimes. He glared at the cast. "Haven't you people memorized your parts?"

Now Zack heard Derek wheeze.

Grimes turned toward the adult actor who would be playing the children's father. "Mr. Woodman?"

"Well, uh, my agent just sent me the script. Last week. Friday, actually."

"And?" inquired Grimes, his left eyebrow arching up nearly to the tip of his pointy hairline.

"Well, I, uh, I haven't really had time to . . ."

"To do your job?"

The actor looked down at his lap.

"What about you?" Grimes snarled at Judy.

"Me?"

"Did you fix those insipid song lyrics?"

"Excuse me? I don't remember you having a problem with any lyrics."

"Then perhaps you weren't listening!"

Zack was ready to whip out his iron fist, but Judy gave him the slightest head shake to let him know she was okay.

"Where exactly do you have a problem, Mr. Grimes?" Judy asked calmly.

He fumbled through his script. "Here. This song. The one Claire sings. Bah! These lyrics need work."

"What kind of work?" asked Judy, refusing to let Grimes bully her, her voice steady and strong.

Grimes narrowed his beady black eyes and looked like he might start hissing steam out both ears like a double-cappuccino machine. "The kind of work that will make it better. Fix it, Mrs. Jennings! I'm sorry if you thought you were coming here on vacation! You are here to work.

Maybe you should send your stepson home so you can concentrate on your job!"

Great. Grimes knew Zack existed. Knew he was in town.

"The rest of you? Go home and memorize your lines! All of them!"

Grimes stood up and stormed out of the room. The man named Hakeem followed him.

Apparently, the table meeting was over.

Zack had intended to tell Judy about the juggling ghost he and Meghan had just bumped into in the stairwell, but from the look on her face, Judy had bigger things to worry about right now.

Like a psycho director who looked ready to explode.

"I'm not sending you home, Zack," Judy said as they waited in the lobby for the elevator, which was working again. "But I am sorry we won't be able to spend as much time together as I thought we would."

"Don't worry. I'll just hang out with Zipper and Meghan."

"You guys are friends already?"

"Yeah. She's neat. Oh, by the way—she loves that song the crazy man just asked you to change."

"Really?"

"Yep. I think Mr. Grimes is just showing off. Acting tough on the first day so everybody will know he's the boss. But this theater wasn't the only one that wanted to do the world premiere of *Curiosity Cat*! There was a bidding war, remember?"

Judy smiled. "So tell me, Zack—how come you always know exactly what to say?"

"I dunno. Maybe I learned it hanging out with you."

The elevator arrived. The sour-faced janitor was riding it. He slid open the accordion cage door.

"Is it working?" Judy asked.

"Aya." The creepy old man stood there and worked his lips around in slow circles like he was gumming a banana. "But you can't take it to the basement."

Judy smiled. "No problem. Our rooms, which, by the way, we do indeed have, are up on the fifth floor."

"Elevator doesn't go to the basement." Now the grizzled old geezer squinted so hard you'd need a topographical map to trace all the craggy lines on his face. "Basement's dark. Scary."

"Right," said Judy. "We're going *up* to five."

"Young person might think he could have all sorts of exciting adventures in the cellar, what with all the costumes and props stored down there. But that young person would be wrong!"

"We're sort of in a hurry," Judy said as sweetly as she could.

"I need to take our dog out for a walk," added Zack.

The janitor waggled a finger. "Don't take your dog to the basement, boy!"

Zack rolled his eyes. "Right. The basement is off-limits. Got it."

Finally, Mr. Kimble stepped off the elevator. Zack and Judy climbed in. She closed the sliding door while Zack punched the button for the fifth floor.

"Going up!" Judy said when they started their smooth ascent.

The janitor stood in the lobby watching them.

"Boy," said Judy. "He must be hiding something pretty incredible down there in the basement!"

30

"Do you have your key?" Grimes asked Hakeem as they hurried through the subterranean labyrinth of interconnected storage rooms in the basement.

"Of course, Exalted One."

They reached the open door to the room where the antique theatrical trunk had been stored.

"Give it to me!" Grimes demanded.

"Not yet."

"What?"

"You are not quite ready to receive it."

"What? I read the book. All of it. I am the direct descendant of the high priest of Ba'al. You shall do as I command!"

Badir and Jamal, the two Tunisian strongmen, stepped into the doorway. Blocked it.

"You are not quite ready," Hakeem repeated, much too serenely for Grimes's taste. "Please . . ." Hakeem gestured toward the door. "Step into the room and learn what is required of you next."

The two musclemen stepped aside, but Grimes could tell they were eyeing him warily.

"No!" he said. "I want you to open that final compartment! Now! You are my servant. You will do as I say!"

Hakeem bent his head in reverence. "I will, Exalted One." He raised his head and glared into Grimes's eyes. "Once you prove that Professor Nicodemus's royal blood truly flows through your veins! That you inherited his natural talents!"

"Who?"

"Professor Nicholas Nicodemus."

"The name embossed on the cover of the book!"

"Indeed. And your grandfather. The world's finest necromancer!"

Grimes had heard the word before. Wasn't quite sure what it meant. For the first time in a long while, he swallowed his pride.

"Necromancer?" he asked as casually as he could.

Hakeem grinned. His eyes twinkled. "One who communicates with the spirits of the dead in order to predict or influence the future."

Badir and Jamal were grinning now, too.

Then the three men started to laugh.

A soft and low, devious and menacing chuckle.

It wasn't long before Grimes was grinning and chuckling with them.

31

"Let's go see what's down there!" said Meghan as soon as Zack told her the janitor's dire warnings about the basement.

They were walking Zipper along the river behind the theater. The little dog was having a great time cataloging all the new scents in this part of Connecticut. He seemed to particularly enjoy Chatham's dandelions.

"Let's go check it out right now!" said Meghan.

"I dunno," said Zack. "He sounded pretty serious."

"Grown-ups always try to scare kids away from stuff they want to keep secret."

"Don't you guys have rehearsal?"

"Nope. Not until tomorrow. I've already memorized all my lines and songs. Come on, Zack. It'll be fun."

"Yeah, but . . ."

Zack couldn't think, thanks to something very loud racing up behind him, making the most annoying sound he'd ever heard. A high-pitched nasal drone. Like a mosquito with a microphone.

Then something hard and pointed and fast slammed into his ankles.

He tripped forward. Scraped his palms when he broke his fall and tumbled sideways.

"Whoops," he heard somebody say. "Sorry."

Zipper was barking, snarling at Zack's unseen attacker: a radio-controlled monster truck with four hulking all-terrain tires the size of hockey pucks.

Derek Stone came running up the path, holding a pistol-grip control unit with an antenna bobbing off the top.

"You okay, kid?" he asked Zack.

Meghan helped Zack to his feet.

"Yeah."

"That's the LST2 monster truck," said Derek as he scooped up his shiny toy. "I tweaked the Mach 427 engine. Haven't quite mastered the steering servos."

"Unh-hunh," said Zack, dusting off his knees.

"So," said Derek, "you guys wanna take a turn?" He held out the controller.

"No thanks," said Meghan.

Zipper barked and wagged his tail.

"Neat dog," said Derek. "Spunky."

"I thought you were allergic," said Zack.

"I am. But I have a prescription." He tucked the truck under his arm so he'd have a free hand to gesture with. "Hey, I won't let allergies stop me from living. I said that once. In a commercial. For a nasal spray."

"Oh, yeah," said Zack. "I saw it on TV."

"Sorry. Can't do an autograph right now. Catch me later."

Zack didn't want to appear rude, so he said, "Okay. Thanks."

"No problem. What's your name again?"

"Zack."

"How do you spell it?"

"Like Jack, only with a Z."

"Weird name," said Derek.

"I guess."

"You should change it." He sneezed. "Excuse me. August. Official start of ragweed season."

"You used to be Derek Frumpkus, right?" Meghan asked.

"That's right. My mom thought Stone had more zazz!"

"Is your mother an actress, too?" Zack asked.

"Used to be. She played a nurse on *Beverly Hills Hospital*."

"Cool," said Zack. "Which nurse?"

"Lots of different ones. She usually only said two or three words. Or pushed the gurney. Or answered the phone in the background."

"Hey, Derek," said Meghan, "want to go on an adventure with us to the basement? You can park your truck at the box office."

"What kind of adventure?"

"A ghost hunt!"

"There's this ghost girl haunting the stairwell," Zack explained. "We think she used to perform here."

"Vaudeville, probably," Meghan added. "She's a juggler."

Derek's eyes bulged. "Ghosts? In the theater?"

"Well, one or two in the stairwell for sure," said Meghan. "The vaudeville girl and some kind of Pilgrim guy who makes a very dramatic entrance!" She yanked up on an imaginary noose and bugged out her eyes. "Aaaack!"

"I saw another one onstage last night," said Zack. "And we think there might be more in the basement, because the janitor keeps telling me not to go down there."

"Ghosts?" Derek's voice cracked.

"Don't worry," said Meghan. "We're bringing the dog."

"Great," Derek said, wheezing.

Zack figured he was allergic to ghosts, too.

32

Wilbur Kimble moved swiftly for an eighty-year-old man.

He draped the crumpled bedsheet against the far wall, propping it up on one side with the tip of a spear, hooking the other end over the antler of a moose head. Both pieces were props from shows done long ago, now stored in the dank basement.

When the children came down here, which Kimble knew they would, because children always did whatever you told them not to do, this sheet would be the first thing they would see.

Actually, what they would see were the wispy images projected on it, a moving picture show that would scare them silly. Children always ran screaming when they encountered the "ghosts" Kimble arranged to have haunting the basement. Usually they cried. Sometimes they had "accidents." Mostly they quit the show and went home.

"Good riddance," he muttered. "This theater is no place for children."

Of course, he himself had never seen a ghost. He just made sure all the kids did.

He pushed apart the dusty costumes hanging on a

rolling wardrobe rack and stepped through the opening to where he had set up the antique movie projector, a relic from the days when the Hanging Hill had been a movie theater back in the 1940s.

"Ran those children out, too," Kimble said, remembering fondly. He had once terrified an entire "Kiddy Matinee" by projecting his spook show on the velvet curtain just before the cartoons started. The popcorn flew that day. Wasn't a dry seat in the house. The theater almost went out of business, which would have been wonderful, might've been torn down for a parking lot.

But some artsy folks with too much time and money decided they wanted to do musicals on the grand old stage and Wilbur Kimble was forced to stay on the job.

He made certain the film sprockets were lined up properly. This was rare footage from the 1930s and needed to be handled very, very carefully. The old celluloid was stiff and brittle.

Kimble flicked up the switch to test out his illusion. The rickety machine chattered to life. The dusty sheet he was using as a movie screen swayed in the slight breeze moving through the basement, and that made the film clip seem all the more like an eerie apparition.

"Clara," the janitor muttered as he watched the ghostly images dance across the sheet: a young girl and boy, dressed up in matching sailor suits.

They tap-danced.

Then they juggled.

First balls, then bowling pins.

33

"If you don't like his changes, don't do them!"

Judy was on the phone with her husband, Zack's dad.

"You need to protect your intellectual property, sweetheart." George Jennings was a lawyer.

"Well, I'm willing to take a look at the lyrics. See if I can make them better."

"You can't. That song is perfect the way it is!"

Judy smiled.

And then George started singing. *"Curiosity helps us see, just how lively life can be. . . ."*

Now Judy was simultaneously laughing and cringing. Her husband was a great guy, a sharp lawyer, and a terrific father. He was also tone-deaf. When he sang, it sounded like a dozen different car horns honking in a barn full of bawling sheep. George Jennings had the kind of voice that could close karaoke bars.

"Okay, okay," said Judy, pulling the phone away from her ear so no permanent nerve damage could be done. "You're right. It's perfect."

"You want me to come down there and sing it to Mr. Grimes? Let him hear just how perfect it is?"

"No, dear."

Judy wouldn't change a word, no matter what the director said.

But she saw no need to torture the poor man.

34

"Ugh! Cobwebs!"

"Come on, Derek," said Meghan. "Don't be a big baby."

"I am not being a baby!"

"Are, too."

"Am not!"

"Whatever."

Zack and Zipper led the way down the staircase spiraling from the lower lobby outside rehearsal room A into the forbidden basement. Meghan was right behind them. Derek brought up the rear.

"Ugh! Moisture!"

Meghan sighed. "Now what?"

"It's dripping!"

Zack looked up at the dimly lit ceiling, where thick steel pipes were strapped to the rafters.

"Relax," said Zack, "it's just water."

"Or," said Meghan, "that could be a sewer line. After all, we are right underneath the men's *lounge*." She leaned into the word so everybody would understand what she really meant: the men's bathroom.

"Raw sewage? I'm allergic to sewage!" Derek pushed

his way past Meghan and Zack, ran down the rest of the stairs, and reached the basement first. "Let's hurry up and get this over with. I don't know what you two expect to find down here."

"We told you," said Meghan. "Ghosts!"

They were directly underneath the main stage. Faint light leaked through the seams between the trapdoors and the floorboards. The vast space was filled with the lumpy shadows of rolling wardrobe racks, wooden storage boxes, and all kinds of furniture and props from shows done long ago.

"There's nothing down here but junk," Derek complained. "Dirty, filthy junk."

"I think it's cool," said Zack. "Like a downstairs attic filled with treasures!"

"I'll bet we discover something incredible," said Meghan, twirling a Chinese parasol she'd just found in a bin.

"Well," said Derek, "all I see are a bunch of old wigs and costumes." He sneezed. "All of them covered with dust." He sneezed again. "I'm allergic to dust."

"What about wool?" Zack asked as they passed a rack crammed with all sorts of coats.

Derek sneezed and scratched his ears. "I'm allergic to just about everything. Wool. Dust. Peanuts. Cats."

"Guess you'd better quit the show," said Meghan.

"Ha-ha. Very funny." Another sneeze.

"I thought you took your allergy medicine," said Meghan.

"Not all of it! I'd be asleep if I did."

They reached the rear wall. To the left was a dark corridor that disappeared under a curving archway. To the right, another passageway.

"That's weird," said Meghan.

"What?" asked Zack.

"Look at all those gloves hanging on the wall!"

"Wow! They're all pointing to the right."

"Oh." Derek scoffed. "Did a ghost do that?"

"Maybe," said Meghan.

"Be difficult," said Zack.

"Oh, really?" whined Derek. "Why's that?"

"Well, ghosts can't move physical objects in the real world," Zack explained.

"Unless," added Meghan, "they get really, really mad or emotional."

Derek snorted a laugh. "Did you two go to Ghost University or something?"

Zack smiled. "Sort of."

Meghan giggled.

"You are both so immature." Derek ignored the finger-pointing gloves and headed down the passageway to the left. Zack and Meghan followed him.

"Ooh. Neat," said Meghan. "It's even darker back here."

"I see a light up ahead," said Zack.

"Yes," said Derek. "It's some sort of . . ."

He froze.

He wheezed.

"Did you just swallow a peanut?" asked Meghan. "Derek?"

Derek stammered something inaudible. All Zack heard was a wispy whimper.

"What is it?"

"Ghosts!" Derek screamed. *"Ghosts!"*

Then he spun around and ran away.

35

Judy took the creaky elevator down to the lobby and marched with great determination to rehearsal room A.

She hoped Reginald Grimes was there. If he wasn't, she'd march up to his office on the second floor.

She was going to tell him, in no uncertain terms, that she wasn't going to change a word of the best song in the whole show.

She pushed open the door.

Grimes wasn't there. Neither was anyone else. The room was empty. Notepads, pencils, and water glasses sat abandoned on the horseshoe of tables where the first read-through of *Curiosity Cat* had never taken place.

Because, Judy thought, *Grimes was too wrapped up in that book he was reading when he should've been working on the show!*

He'd left the book behind.

It was sitting in the middle of the head table.

Judy tiptoed over. She wasn't exactly sure why she was tiptoeing. It just felt like she was snooping.

The book had a crinkled leather cover. A frightening

image of a snorting bull had been scorched into the center with a branding iron.

LIBRARY OF PROFESSOR NICHOLAS NICODEMUS was embossed in chipped gold letters in the lower right corner.

Judy reached out to open the book.

She snapped back her hand as soon as she heard the door swing open behind her.

The man named Hakeem, Grimes's assistant, scurried into the rehearsal room.

"Ah! There it is!" he said. "Just where Mr. Grimes left it."

He snatched the big book off the table, turned on his heel, and hurried out the door before Judy could ask him anything.

Like *Who the heck is Professor Nicholas Nicodemus?*

36

Zack and Meghan stood mesmerized by what they saw shimmering on the far wall.

"Cool," said Meghan.

"Yeah," Zack agreed.

It was a young girl and boy, both wearing costumes that sort of made them look like that sailor on the front of a Cracker Jack box.

Both juggling fruit.

"They're pretty good," whispered Zack. He didn't recognize the boy, but the girl sure looked familiar. She was the one he and Meghan had seen juggling in the stairwell. Only, she wasn't.

"She's not real," said Zack.

"That's her," said Meghan.

"Yeah. Only it's not *really* her. She's—I don't know— too flat." Zack held a finger to his lips. "Hear it?"

"Yeah," said Meghan.

The faint whir of a movie projector.

Zack took a top hat off a Styrofoam head and blew away the dust rimming its brim. Soon tiny flecks were sparkling in the movie projector's narrow funnel of light.

Zipper made his way to where the beacon disappeared through the costumes hanging on a wardrobe rack, and Zack thought about that scene in *The Wizard of Oz* where Toto pulls open the curtains to reveal the humbug pretending to be a wizard. Today it was Zipper's turn. He chomped into a gown and yanked it sideways.

Meghan lunged at the rack with a rubber-tipped tomahawk, another prop from another show.

"Hiyah!" She attacked the empty clothes. "Hiyah!"

"Meghan?"

"Nothing," she reported. "Nobody."

Zack peered through the opening and saw an unattended movie projector unspooling a reel of film.

"Somebody set this up," he said. "Hung that sheet against the wall to make a movie screen."

"Why?"

Zack shrugged. "Maybe they like old juggler movies."

"Yeah, you don't see many of those at the multiplex anymore."

All of a sudden, they heard the sharp *swick-swick-swick* of a swishing sword.

" 'A hit, a very palpable hit!' "

Zipper dropped to his belly, assumed his pounce position.

Zack and Meghan pushed apart the costumes and peered out at a dashing young man in tights, a tunic, and what looked like balloon-legged shorts. He was flicking his rapier back and forth, fencing with an unseen enemy.

"'Another hit; what say you?' 'A touch, a touch, I do confess!'"

"That's the swordfight scene from *Hamlet*," Meghan whispered. "He's doing all the parts!"

The guy was fit and trim, with long dark hair that swept back over the puffy shoulders of his costume. He waggled his blade with one hand while the other remained heroically cocked at his hip. Zack figured he must've been a leading man or a movie star. Maybe both.

"'O villainy!' Ho!" He clutched his chest. "'Thou hast slain me!'" He staggered forward. "'Cowards die many times before their deaths; the valiant ne'er taste of death but once.'" He dropped to his knees. "I . . . am . . . done . . . for."

And then he vanished

"He's a ghost," said Zack. "A *real* one!"

"He's also a ham," said Meghan. "I've never seen anybody chew that much scenery in one bite."

"Help!"

"That's Derek!" said Zack.

"Help! It's a giant! A giant monster!"

Zack and Meghan looked at each other.

"Cool!"

They'd track down the missing projectionist later. Right now they had to go rescue Derek Stone from some sort of Giant Monster!

No wonder Kimble didn't want kids in the basement. It was more fun than Disney World!

37

"You bolted the doors?" Hakeem asked his two associates.

They nodded.

"The janitor?"

"Working elsewhere."

Hakeem now turned to Grimes. "When is your next scheduled performance?"

"This afternoon. Three p.m."

"Good. We have time. Several hours."

"For what?"

"Your audition, Exalted One. Please. Let us form a circle."

The three Tunisian men held hands.

Great, Grimes thought, *they want me to play ring-around-the-rosy. Right here at center stage. On the darkened set of Dracula's castle.*

"Please, Exalted One. Take our hands. Form a circle with us around this lamp. We must be positioned over the portal."

Somewhat reluctantly, Grimes reached out with his right hand and clutched the extended left hand of the giant named Badir.

While he did, Hakeem reached over and took hold of Grimes's left. Elevated his crippled arm. The pain washed up through the shoulder socket, then drifted away.

"Tighten the circle, gentlemen," Hakeem said, and the four men shuffled closer to the ghost light. The caged bulb was exceedingly bright. At least five hundred watts. Grimes feared it might fry a permanent dot onto his retina.

"Tell me, Exalted One," said Hakeem, "have you ever sensed that you might possess the power to bring back the spirit of one long since departed? To summon forth the souls of the dead?"

Grimes shook his head. Answered honestly. "No. I don't think so."

"Think hard."

"No. I never . . ."

Jinx!

The cat. Yesterday. Had he brought back the spirit of his long-dead friend simply by wishing for it?

"My cat," he whispered. "Maybe."

The other men sighed and nodded.

"This is good," said Hakeem. "Very good. You might, indeed, be blessed with your grandfather's gifts."

Hearing that caused Grimes to stand a little taller, his chest to swell. "Well, I suppose it's possible. Maybe a little."

"We shall see. Badir? Anoint the ground!"

The big man broke the circle so he could reach into a pouch he carried slung over his shoulder. He started to sprinkle dirt at their feet.

"What's that?" Grimes asked.

"Earth. From a graveyard. Jamal?"

Now Jamal let go of the hands he was holding and produced a cloth sack.

"Eat!" he said, presenting Grimes with a stale slice of black bread.

Grimes ate. It was dry and tasteless.

"Drink!" Out came a small corked vial containing purple liquid.

"What is it?" Grimes asked.

"Unfermented grape juice," answered Hakeem.

Grimes drank. The juice was sour. Needed sugar.

Now Jamal unwrapped a sheet of butcher paper from around a slab of gray meat resembling jerky.

"Am I to eat this as well?" Grimes asked.

"Yes," said Hakeem. "It is the final course."

Grimes took the meat from Jamal. "What is the meaning behind all this?"

"These are all food items associated with the underworld. The realm of the dead."

Grimes nodded. Chewed on the tough, stringy meat.

"Unleavened black bread!" Hakeem declared. "Without yeast, it is lifeless and black like the shroud of death. Grape juice! To honor Dionysus, the Greek god of the vine. One of the few ancient deities able to ferry dead souls up from the underworld!"

Grimes nodded. The symbolism made sense. "And this final course? The meat?"

"To pay patronage to Hecate, goddess of sorcery, you must eat her favored earthly animal. You must eat flesh from the corpse of a dead dog!"

He wished he hadn't asked.

38

Meghan, Zack, and Zipper backtracked, made their way up the dimly lit maze of corridors.

Zipper barked.

"Lead the way, Zip!"

The dog took off.

"See, Zack?" said Meghan. "I told you we'd have an adventure down here!"

"We should've brought a flashlight!"

"What about that? That magic fairy wand or whatever. Maybe the star lights up." She pulled the prop wand out of its bin. "There's a switch on the handle." She flipped it back and forth. Nothing happened. "Batteries must be dead."

"Whack it on the bottom a couple times. It's how I get my flashlight to work at home."

Meghan whacked it.

The sparkling star glowed.

"Help!" Derek's voice was weaker now.

"Hang on!" shouted Zack.

"We're coming!" added Meghan.

They rounded a final corner and raced down a steep ramp that switched back a couple of times before it entered a storage vault at least fifty feet tall and wide.

"So, the basement has a basement!" said Meghan. "It's probably where they store the *huge* set pieces. Then they use a freight elevator or something to hoist stuff up to the stage."

"Zack!" Derek whimpered. "Tell your dog to stop licking me!"

Meghan swung her wand light to the right.

Derek was cowering on the cement floor, trying to cover up with his elbows so Zipper couldn't slobber all over his face.

Zack stared up at the giant creature that had terrified Derek.

"Wow!"

It had to be at least twelve feet tall. A gargantuan brass statue of a man who had the head of a bull. Mr. Bull Head was seated on a throne with his hands held out in front of him, palms up, like he was waiting for someone to toss him a basketball.

"I couldn't see where I was going and bumped into that thing!" Derek explained. "When I looked up . . ."

"You screamed like a baby," said Meghan. "Don't worry. I would've done the same thing."

"Yeah. Me too," said Zack. "This guy's got some nasty nostrils."

All three of them studied the colossus.

"I wonder what show they used it in," said Meghan.

"Was there ever a *Bulls*?" asked Derek. "You know, like *Cats*?"

"I don't think so," said Meghan. "It's so huge! It looks like it might be from an opera."

Zack heard someone sobbing.

From the look on her face, he could tell that Meghan heard it, too.

"What's wrong?" Derek asked.

"Someone's crying," said Zack.

Derek looked at them both like they were crazy. "What? Where?"

Meghan and Zack both held a finger up to their lips, urged Derek to keep quiet.

He stayed where he was.

They crept around the brass man's big sandaled feet. Zipper padded along after them

Whatever was behind the statue wouldn't stop weeping.

39

The four men stood holding hands in a circle around the ghost light at center stage.

Grimes wished he had a toothbrush. He still tasted the canine carcass.

"Repeat after me," Hakeem instructed. *"Ego sum te peto et videre queo!"*

"That's Latin."

"Of course."

"Well, what does it mean?"

"Did you not read *The Book of Ba'al*?"

Grimes hesitated. "I skimmed some sections."

"So I feared. *Ego sum te peto et videre queo:* I seek you and demand to see you."

"I seek you and demand to see you."

"In Latin, please."

"Ego sum te peto et videre queo."

"Louder."

"Ego sum te peto et videre queo!"

"Again!"

"Whose spirit are we summoning?"

"Let us start at the top of your grandfather's list. Mad Dog Murphy."

"Who's he?"

"Convicted bank robber. Murderer. Died in the electric chair in 1959."

"What do we want with him?"

"Repeat the words."

"First you tell me why we would want a murdering bank robber!"

"Because he is very good at his job!" said Hakeem. The other two men sniggered. "Repeat the words!"

Grimes felt the warmth of power surging through his body. Jolts of adrenaline rippled up from his hands as he clutched the hands of the two brothers of Hannibal. Who were these people? Why did they make him feel like he could soar through the air like an eagle, commanding all those below? Like his lame arm would somehow grow strong enough to wield a terrible swift sword and fell any who stood in his way?

"*Ego sum te peto et videre queo!*" he cried "Mad Dog Murphy! I seek you and demand to see you!"

"Louder!"

"I seek you and demand to see you! Now!"

The bulb atop the ghost light exploded.

Sparks arced up from the exposed filament.

Electricity crackled across the air, igniting a roaring thunderclap. Four lightning bolts collided at center stage with the screech of steel wheels screaming to a stop in a train wreck.

A monstrous man strapped in a wooden chair suddenly materialized in the air. He floated ten feet above the floor, bobbing like a tossed boat on a churning sea.

"Where am I?" the beast in the chair bellowed.

"Are you the spirit of Mad Dog Murphy?" Grimes demanded.

"Yeah, yeah. Sure. Where the blazes am I?"

"Where I summoned you!" answered Grimes, feeling more robust and vital than he had ever felt in his life.

He was his grandfather's rightful heir.

He was a true necromancer!

Zack heard a muffled boom somewhere right above his head.

He figured it must be a summer thunderstorm.

He and Meghan and Zipper continued creeping around the base of the giant brass statue.

They reached the back.

The girl hidden in the darkness continued to sob and moan and weep.

Meghan flicked on her illuminated wand.

A young Native American girl, maybe twelve, stood in the shadows, tears streaming down her face. She wore a fringed buckskin dress decorated with beadwork, and cradled a dozen ears of dried corn tight against her chest.

"Are you a demon?" she asked Zack in a quavering voice.

Zack shook his head.

The girl turned toward Meghan. Shook and sobbed. "Are you a demon?"

"No. I'm Meghan. Meghan McKenna. Who are you?"

The girl couldn't answer. She convulsed into another spasm of sobs.

"What's wrong?" asked Zack. "Does something hurt? Are you in pain?"

The weeping girl nodded. As she did, her head seemed sort of loose and rubbery on her neck.

Zack glanced down at the floor. The girl was standing in the center of an area squared off by the stumps of four rough beams. Maybe sawed-off support posts from an old foundation. Wormy six-by-sixes.

Now he heard footsteps.

"Hey . . . who are you guys talking to back here?" It was Derek.

"My father curses this ground!" the girl cried out. It was hard to understand what she was saying, because she kept sobbing the whole time she talked. "I did not steal this corn! We gave you demons the seed; how could we steal that which we gave you?"

Zack wished he knew the answer, but he didn't, so he gave the ghost a pleading shrug. Meghan did the same thing.

Zipper sank to the floor and whimpered.

The girl wailed the most mournful cry Zack had ever heard in his life, worse than a million funerals all mixed together.

Then she and her corn crumbled into powdery dust and disappeared.

"Wow," said Meghan.

"Yeah," said Zack.

"We have to find out who she was."

"Who *who* was?" asked Derek. He was staring at Zack, Meghan, and even Zipper as if all three were deranged.

"The girl," said Zack.

"What girl?"

"In the buckskin dress?" said Meghan.

"She was just here," said Zack.

"When?"

"Two seconds ago," said Meghan.

"Ha-ha. Very funny. Can we go back upstairs now?"

Zack and Meghan looked at each other and realized Derek Stone couldn't see ghosts!

41

Reginald Grimes sat onstage, slumped in a cushioned chair with snarling skulls carved into its armrests.

He was exhausted. Drained. Necromancy was tough work. It seemed the ritual sapped some of his life force and transferred it to the souls he summoned up from the dead.

"Where did Mr. Murphy go?" Grimes mumbled weakly.

Hakeem indicated the general vicinity of the air. "His spirit is now free to roam the theater, to haunt its dark and dismal places until such time as you command him to return to the nether regions below."

"He comes and goes at my bidding?"

"Yes, Exalted One."

"I see. And this makes me rich and powerful beyond my wildest dreams how?"

Hakeem smiled. "All in good time."

"Bah!" snapped Grimes. "So you keep saying. However, I grow weary of your tedious retorts, these tiresome rituals. Not to mention the foul-tasting dog jerky! I want to know what's locked in the final drawer of that show trunk, and I want to know now!"

Hakeem bowed obsequiously. "Patience is a virtue, Exalted One."

"Well, I'm tired of being virtuous. I demand to know what you are keeping hidden from me!"

"Soon. First, you must also master the art of necyomancy."

Grimes squinted. "Nec-*yo*-mancy?"

"Indeed," said Hakeem. "It is very similar to nec-*ro*-mancy but much more difficult. In necyomancy, you can call forth demons more wretchedly powerful than Mr. Mad Dog Murphy."

"Demons?"

"The devil in human disguise. Souls of the purest evil."

"I see."

"However," said Hakeem, holding up a hand in warning, "if necyomancy is done incorrectly, those summoned can quickly turn against the summoner."

"And tell me: Did my grandfather also provide a list of evil entities to be beckoned forth from the deepest recesses of the underworld?"

"He did."

Grimes rolled his good hand, gesturing for more information. "Go on. Give me a name."

"Diamond Mike Butler. The Butcher Thief of Bleecker Street."

"Is he a true demon?"

"It is why they called him the Butcher. Mr. Butler was a jewel thief who liked to burglarize the homes of the wealthy late at night so he could slay any children he found asleep in their beds. He used a meat cleaver. Chopped off their small heads. When spirits this vile are called back . . ." Hakeem hesitated.

"What?" Grimes demanded.

"They return more monstrous than when they were alive!"

"Did my grandfather ever dare to summon forth this monstrous soul?"

"Yes. Several times. However, he always sent him back to the underworld very quickly."

Grimes stood from the chair. "Really? Well, gentlemen, let's rejoin hands. We don't want to keep Mr. Butler waiting. I'm sure he's quite eager to make his triumphant return to the stage!"

Judy returned to the fifth floor.

She couldn't find Reginald Grimes. The company manager said he was tied up in meetings with the producers for the rest of the day.

Fine. It was almost one-thirty and she was getting a hunger headache. If Zack was done playing with Zipper and his new friends, maybe they could go grab a sandwich at the diner across the street.

She entered her room and went to the door connecting her half of the suite with Zack's.

"Zack? Are you in there? Zack, honey?"

She heard a crash. It sounded like glass shattering.

"Zack? Are you okay?"

No answer.

"Did something break, honey?"

Nothing.

She fumbled with the doorknob and realized it was locked on the other side.

"Hang on, honey."

Judy went out into the hallway, where she saw a tall,

slender woman with curly hair walking away from Zack's bedroom door.

"Excuse me," Judy said. The woman kept walking. She said it more loudly: "Excuse me?"

The woman drifted down the hall toward the stairwell.

"Were you just in my son's room?"

No answer.

Judy hurried to Zack's door. Jiggled the knob. It was locked.

"Zack? Are you in there? Zack?"

"Hey, Mom."

Judy whirled around to see Zack and Zipper stepping off the elevator.

"What's up?" he asked.

Judy turned to see if the woman with the curly hair was still walking down the hall.

She wasn't.

She had vanished.

Wilbur Kimble hurried back to the basement.

The audience would start arriving for the Sunday matinee soon. Time to put things away downstairs.

Earlier, from his hiding place, he had watched the blond boy run away while the other two children discovered his movie projector. The imitation ghosts didn't seem to frighten those two in the slightest. In fact, the encounter only seemed to make them more curious.

Just like that blasted cat in the new musical.

No, these two children would not be easy to run off. He would need to speak directly with Clara.

He went into a cramped, windowless closet, closed and locked the door. He struck a match and lit a small fluttering candle so the room wouldn't be completely dark. He placed the candle next to his antique Ouija board on an upturned apple crate.

Kimble creaked down into a folding chair and placed his fingertips atop the Ouija's planchette—a small heart-shaped piece of wood with a glass eye in its center that acted as a movable indicator so the board could spell out messages from the great beyond. It was the only way he knew to communicate with the dead.

"Weird and mysterious Ouija," Kimble muttered, "allow me to speak once more with Clara."

He closed his eyes and waited.

"Clara, can you hear me?" he asked.

He felt the pointer begin to glide, up and to the left, skating across the board to the smiling sun and the word "YES."

Kimble maneuvered the reader back to the center.

"Clara, have you seen the children who recently arrived here?"

He waited. Felt another tug. Let the heart-shaped pointer move where it wanted to move.

YES.

"Clara," he whispered, "the moon is nearly full! Do you realize what danger these youngsters bring with them?"

Once again, the reader took his hands to the upper left corner.

YES.

He pulled the pointer back to the center.

"Will you help me scare them off?"

The reader did not move.

"Clara? Will you help me rid this theater of its children?"

Suddenly, the pointer zipped up to the far *right* corner.

The scowling quarter moon. The Dog Star. Billowing black clouds.

NO.

Kimble pressed down hard, tried to drag the reader back to the center. It wouldn't budge.

"Please!" He exerted more pressure, made his fingertips tremble with the effort.

The reader remained glued to "NO."

"Clara? Please!"

"Clara isn't here, pops."

Kimble looked up and nearly had a heart attack.

There was a man strapped into an electric chair sitting on the opposite side of the apple crate.

"You shouldn't play Ouija in the dark, pops. You do, you might start seeing ghosts!" The man tossed back his head and laughed. The air in the cramped closet reeked of hot, rotting beef.

"Who are you?"

"Mad Dog Murphy. I kill people."

Kimble sprang for the door. Tried to slide his key into the lock. His hands were trembling.

"Drop it!" Mad Dog's fetid breath came at Kimble like a gust of wind blasting up from a sewer grate. It blew out the flickering candle.

That startled Kimble, made him flinch, made him drop his key.

He heard it clink against something metal, then rattle and clank its way down a pipe.

He had dropped the key into a floor drain. He was trapped inside an unlit closet.

"Give it up, old-timer," said the man in the chair as bursts of blindingly white light flared up from his metal skullcap. "You can't talk to Clara! Not now, not never again!" Another laugh. More stench. "What's that old saying? When one door closes, another door opens? Too bad it ain't gonna be that closet door. It's gonna be ours! The doorway of the damned is all set to swing wide open, pops! Tomorrow night! Tomorrow night!"

Zack found his room key and opened the door.

"I heard something fall over here," said Judy. "A crash."

"Yep." Zack pointed to the shards of shattered glass near his chest of drawers. "I packed a picture. Guess it must've fallen off the dresser."

Judy bent down and picked up the photograph underneath the sheet of splintered glass. It was a snapshot of the new Jennings family: Judy, George, Zack, and Zipper.

"Well," said Judy, "the photograph isn't damaged. We can always buy a new frame."

"Wonder how come it fell."

"Me too," said Judy, standing up. "Did you put it near the edge?"

"Nope. I put it on top, right there in the middle."

"And the window's closed, so a breeze didn't knock it over."

"Judy?"

"Yes, Zack?"

"I think we might have ghosts again."

"Really?"

"Yeah. I saw some stuff downstairs in the basement."

"You went where the janitor told you not to?"

"Sorry."

Judy smiled. "I would've done the same thing."

"Meghan McKenna told me every theater she's ever worked in was haunted. Probably because there's so many emotions stirred up inside 'em. Plus, you know actors. If they have a good part, they never want to leave the stage."

"Meghan might be right. I just saw a very strange lady walking down the hall. Actually, it looked like she was *gliding* down the hall."

"You know, Mom, you're one of the few adults who can see ghosts during the day."

"Lucky me. I think she may have come in here, even though both doors were locked."

"Probably oozed her way in."

"Then she walked out—right through the wall."

"Was she juggling?" Zack asked.

"No. No juggling. Just, you know, silently drifting."

"One of the ghosts Meghan and I met juggles."

"Really?"

"Yeah. Mostly in the stairwell."

"I see."

"Another one is a Pilgrim. He hangs himself. Then there's the actress who comes onstage for her standing ovation, and the Shakespearean actor with the sword, and the sad Indian girl. . . ."

"You and Meghan McKenna have seen that many ghosts?"

"Well, she hasn't seen the Pilgrim guy or the actress taking her bows."

"But Meghan sees ghosts? Like we do?"

"Yep. But Derek doesn't."

They finished picking up the broken glass and tossed the pieces into a wicker trash basket.

"So, do you think it was a ghost lady who knocked the picture frame off the dresser?"

"I don't know, Zack. The ghosts back in North Chester couldn't really *do* anything, remember?"

"True. But I've read that if they concentrate all their energy, if they get, let's say, really mad or incredibly sad, they can rattle chains and push stuff around."

"You've been reading books about ghosts?"

"Sure. After that night in the crossroads, haven't you?"

"Yeah. About a dozen. Everything the library had." Judy stared at the door. "Wow. I wonder who she was."

"Just another actress who never heard her cue to exit. So, you hungry?"

"Starving."

"I told Meghan that we might join her and her mother across the street at the diner."

"Great." Judy remembered something else from back at the crossroads. "Your new friend Meghan's not a ghost, is she?"

"Nah. I saw her eat a hunk out of a doughnut this morning."

"Good."

He hears the ancient command: *Ego sum te peto et videre queo.*

"I seek you and demand to see you."

He hears his name being called.

"I seek you, Michael Butler, and demand to see you."

He zooms up through the gloom. Races toward the light.

He sees the new necromancer. Faintly. Dimly. As if he were looking at the man through a gauzy veil.

"You will find me to be a stern but benevolent master, Mr. Butler!" the sorcerer declares. "You may remain in this realm until four a.m. Then you must return below and await further instructions! Do you understand?"

He nods.

"Excellent!" the new master decrees. "Soon I will send you out to do my bidding!"

Fascinating.

Maybe this new necromancer intends to give him back his body.

Maybe this time he will be fully restored to life.

Maybe he will once again be able to do all the things he used to do!

Maybe he will be able to kill again.

Judy and Zack sat with Meghan and her mother at a diner table with chrome legs and a speckled top.

"You're Meghan McKenna!" said a fan about thirteen years old, trembling near their table, flapping a napkin and a pen.

Meghan smiled. "Hi. Would you like an autograph?"

"Yes! Ohmigoodness!" The fan had just recognized Judy, too. "You're Judy Magruder! I've read all your books!"

Judy's turn to smile. "Do you have another napkin?"

"Here," said Mrs. McKenna. "You can use mine. Nobody ever asks for the mother's autograph."

"Or the stepson's," said Zack.

"Guess we're just not very interesting, hunh?"

"True. But we do get to eat first!"

After Judy had signed about a dozen napkins (to Meghan's fifty), she watched Zack and Meghan devour their late lunch, made even later by the flurry of fans that descended on their table once word hit the street that Meghan McKenna was "inside eating!" Both kids wolfed

145

down hamburgers and french fries from tissue-lined baskets and sucked hard on extraordinarily thick chocolate milk shakes. The talented young movie star had quite an appetite; Judy was confident she wasn't a ghost.

"So," Judy said to Mrs. McKenna, "is this your first trip to Connecticut?"

"No. Meghan did a movie here once. Something about a horse."

"*Fredericka the Faithful Filly,*" said Meghan.

"Don't talk with you mouth full of food, honey."

"Sorry."

"Your daughter's a terrific actress," said Judy. "I wasn't surprised when she was nominated for an Oscar."

Mrs. McKenna shrugged. "She's having fun. As soon as it isn't fun . . ."

"We're done!" said Meghan, dabbing at her lips with a napkin.

"Meghan has a gift," said Mrs. McKenna. "However, I refuse to become a stage mother, making my kid miserable by dragging her off to auditions when she'd rather be home playing soccer in the mud. I will not live vicariously through my daughter's triumphs."

"What's 'vicariously'?" asked Zack.

Meghan raised her hand and answered: "Vicariously: Experienced through another person, rather than firsthand."

"Very good," said Mrs. McKenna. "I'm glad to see you studied your vocabulary words. However, we still have math homework to do tonight. Science, too."

"Yes, Mom."

"You're Meghan's teacher?" asked Judy.

"When she's on the road, which it seems like we have been for over a year. Before my daughter became an actress, I taught middle school. My husband still does."

"You still teach, too, Mom," said Meghan.

"Yes, but only one student in a one-room school-house," Mrs. McKenna said warmly. "Typically a hotel room or trailer near a movie set. I have my master's degree in history."

"I'm impressed," said Judy.

"Don't be. It's why we almost didn't do your show."

Now she was confused. "What do you mean?"

"Well," said Mrs. McKenna hesitantly, "let's just say the Hanging Hill Playhouse does not have a very good history when it comes to productions featuring children."

"Really?"

"*The Music Man* was the last show they did with any children in the cast and it closed after two performances because the young actor playing the part of Winthrop refused to come out of his dressing room!"

"Why?"

"There are rumors that the theater is haunted."

Judy pretended to be surprised. "Is that so?"

"I did a little research. Dug up all sorts of stories about frightening 'presences.' Stage lights going on and off by themselves. Footsteps and voices up on the catwalks when nobody's there. Odd breezes and odors. There's even an actress named Thelma Beaumont who died of a heart attack, right at center stage when the audience rose to give her a standing ovation. They say she keeps coming back to take one more curtain call."

There was a clink.

"Sorry." Zack had just dropped his fork.

"Even Mr. Justus Willowmeier the Third is rumored to show up from time to time."

"Is he the one who built the Hanging Hill Publick House?" asked Judy.

"No, he was *that* Willowmeier's grandson and the one who transformed the hotel and tavern into an entertainment emporium. Justus the Third loved show people. Particularly show*girls*. He was seldom seen without a cigar in his mouth and a pretty woman on each arm. He also kept one of the apartments on the top floor. Liked to host rowdy parties up there, and according to several of the stories, he still does!"

"That's where we're staying," said Judy. "The top floor."

"Us too. Maybe, if we're lucky, we'll all get invited to one of his cast parties!"

"So all these ghostly presences scare the kids away?"

"Yep."

"I wonder why the theater wanted to do my show," said Judy.

"Maybe because your script only needs two children," said Mrs. McKenna. "But—I'll be honest—if Meghan didn't love your books so much, well, we wouldn't be here."

"Why?"

Mrs. McKenna took in a deep breath. "Seventy years ago," she said, "a child performer died here. A girl."

Judy was horrified. "In a show?"

"I'm not sure. My information right now is sort of sketchy. Got it from Florence, the ninety-year-old sweetheart who volunteers in the box office. Anyway, Florence told me there was a fire 'of suspicious origin' back in the late 1930s and she vaguely remembers the police arresting a man, one of the touring vaudeville performers, charging him with arson and first-degree felony murder."

"Oh my."

"The little girl who died in the blaze was also on the vaudeville bill. Part of a brother-sister juggling act."

Now there were two clinks.

This time, both Zack *and* Meghan had dropped their forks.

Right after lunch, Zack and Judy went with Meghan and her mom to the three p.m. Sunday matinee of *Bats in Her Belfry.*

Meghan and Judy had to sign a bunch more autographs before they could sit down.

Zack and Mrs. McKenna did not.

Zack thought the show was pretty neat. Dracula made an extremely cool entrance—floating down through a huge window in his castle. Since it was a musical *comedy,* the window wasn't open.

The renowned vampire hunter Van Helsing attempted to expose the smooth and debonair count by inviting him to a big banquet where all they served was spaghetti in garlic sauce and garlic bread. One neat scene showed Dracula getting locked in his coffin, which was then chained inside a concrete crypt like in a magic show. Some townspeople turned the box around and around and it didn't look like there was any way for the actor to escape through trapdoors in the floor, because the crypt was on an elevated platform, but when the vampire hunters undid the chains, all they found inside the tomb was a single dead rose.

In the second act, the lady playing Lucy, one of the women falling in love with Dracula, started singing that "Bitten and Smitten" song Judy had sung in the car.

She wasn't alone.

Every move she made and every note she sang was mirrored by a second woman wearing a slightly different costume and wig. They were only inches apart and moving in complete sync across the stage—like those swimmers at the Olympics. Zack thought this was hilarious.

Except he realized: Nobody in the audience was laughing.

Maybe because they couldn't see the Lucy double.

He turned to Meghan on his right.

"Yep," she whispered. "It's a ghost."

He turned to Judy on his left.

"It's Kathleen Williams," she whispered. "From the original cast! She's really good, isn't she?"

Yeah, Zack thought. *Especially for a dead person.*

After Summoning Murphy, Butler, and several other deceased criminal masterminds, Grimes and the Tunisians had taken a four-hour break from conjuring demons, vacating the stage just before the Sunday-afternoon performance of *Bats in Her Belfry*.

Immediately after the matinee, however, when the audience was gone, the lobby was empty, and the doors were once again barred, Reginald Grimes returned to center stage to form a necromancy circle with the three other men.

"Who's next?" he asked Hakeem without much enthusiasm.

"Lilly Pruett."

The name sounded familiar. A distant childhood memory. Something to do with girls skipping rope.

His mind was wandering. Grimes was exhausted. Dead tired. He couldn't remember half of the names of the spirits he had summoned up from the underworld.

"She was originally summoned by the professor," Hakeem explained. "Now she must answer to you!"

"How much more of this must I endure before you unlock the trunk's final compartment?"

Hakeem unfurled a long scroll filled with names. "Fortunately, a few of the spirits your grandfather was familiar with still reside here in the theater. William Bampfield . . ."

"Bampfield? Who's he?"

"An early settler. A Pilgrim, I believe you call them. He stole his neighbor's cattle, killed his wife and two daughters. Claimed the devil told him to do it. Went to the gallows."

"Wonderful," Grimes said sarcastically. "And what, pray tell, do I want with him?"

"Mr. Bampfield should prove most eager to steal and kill again."

"So?"

"He'd be delighted to do so for *you*. To kill, to rob, to pillage, plunder, pilfer, ransack, and loot. So would they all. These evil spirits will do anything you ask of them. They simply need a good director to tell them where to go and what to do."

"Wait a minute," said Grimes. "You're telling me these ghosts can actually rob banks, steal diamonds, forge checks, embezzle funds, make me rich beyond my wildest dreams and kill anyone who tries to stop us?"

"Yes. Not now. But soon."

"Bah! You keep saying that. 'Soon! Soon!' How soon?"

"Tomorrow. When the moon is full. When the sacred ceremony is complete."

"What ceremony?"

"The one you will perform with the two children!"

"Really? And, tell me, Hakeem: What's in all this for you?"

Hakeem smiled. "Enough gold and treasure to restore Carthage to its full and rightful glory! It is all we brothers of Hannibal have ever dreamed of for over two thousand years! You, oh high priest of Ba'al, you shall make our dreams at long last come true!"

Zack had taken Zipper out for a walk right before he and Judy had called it a night and gone to bed—Judy to her room, Zack and Zipper to his.

Now Zipper was nudging Zack with his snout.

Apparently, the dog needed to go out again.

"Mmmfff." Zack buried his head under his pillow.

Zipper kept nuzzling, burrowing into the blankets, and prying the pillow away from Zack's face so he could lick it.

"What time is it?" Zack mumbled.

Rubbing his eyes and sitting up, Zack found his watch on the bedside table.

3:55 a.m.

Zipper nose-nudged him, poked him in the ribs.

"Okay, Zip. I get it."

Too bad they weren't at home, where Zack could just open the back door and let Zip out into the yard to do his business. Here in Chatham, if Zipper had to take another pee, Zack had to walk him down five floors to the lobby.

Zack put on his glasses. Slipped on his bathrobe and sneakers. He didn't bother tying up the laces.

"Come on, Zip." Yawning, he snapped the leash onto the dog's collar.

They headed out the door, moved down the hallway past Judy's room. Zack shuffled while Zipper padded. They made their way to the elevator. Zack pressed the call button, heard its motor whir.

"At least the elevator's running," Zack said through another jaw-stretcher of a yawn.

Zipper wagged his tail and smiled up at him: a dog's way of saying "sorry to wake you up, pal" and "thanks for taking me out."

"No problem-o," said Zack, bending down to scratch Zipper behind the ears. "Just hold it until we get outside, okay?" Zack definitely did not want to deal with any grief from that scraggly old janitor if Zipper had an accident.

The elevator squealed to a stop. Zack slid open the accordion cage door.

Someone was inside. Weeping.

"Are you a demon?" she asked.

The Native American girl was standing inside the elevator.

She was still sobbing.

"The corn is ours!" she blubbered. "How can we steal what is ours?"

Suddenly, Zack heard a tremendous whoosh.

Someone else shot up the elevator shaft: Streaming through the floor of the car was a blast of dust that materialized into a person who clutched a sparkling necklace in one hand and brandished a bloody meat cleaver in the other.

"Silence, little girl, or I promise: I shall give you something to cry about!"

The girl wailed louder.

"Silence, I said!"

The new ghost was dressed in a black top hat and a Dracula-style cape. Blood was spattered all over his white shirt and waistcoat. Blood was caked on the blade of his cleaver.

Zipper whimpered.

Zack wished he had taken the time to tie his shoelaces; it would've made running away easier.

"My time is nearly up!" Cleaver Man cried. "But I shall return! Oh, yes—I shall return!" He disappeared.

The girl stopped crying.

Zack heard that trapdoor sound again.

The Indian girl fell halfway through the solid floor, then stopped with a jerk. Her head snapped sideways. She gacked and a bloated black tongue popped out of her mouth.

"Come on, Zip!"

Zack scooped up his dog and bolted down the hall to the stairwell.

Zipper still had to pee.

That meant Zack still had to face whoever or whatever else might be lurking in the shadows on the five flights of steps they would need to descend before they reached the lobby.

He just hoped whomever they bumped into wouldn't be as scary as the girl swinging from an invisible noose back in the elevator.

Or the Jack the Ripper look-alike who popped in with his jewelry and bloody butcher blade.

Zack was whistling.

He figured that if it worked when walking past grave-yards, it might work in haunted stairwells, too.

"Five more floors to go," he whispered tensely to Zipper.

The stairwell was windowless and nearly dark, illuminated only by the soft red glow of Exit signs on every landing. Zack kept one hand on the cold handrail, used it to feel his way down the steps; his other arm was wrapped snugly around Zipper.

He heard a *tick-tick-tick*.

Something was clicking. He stopped. The sound stopped, too.

Juggler Girl, he thought. *Plastic balls!*

Zipper squirmed in his arms. Zack could see that pained sorry-but-I-really-have-to-pee look in his eyes.

"Okay. Hang on."

He headed down the steps again. Faster.

The *tick-tick-tick* started up again. Faster. Zack figured the girl was spinning her balls like crazy, getting warmed up to attack.

He rounded the third-floor landing.

Tick-tick-tick-tick-tick.

What if she was juggling knives with plastic handles? Magician's knives!

Tick-tick-tick.

What if, defying all the rules, her ghostly knives could actually hurt a human and a dog?

Zack stopped.

So did the ticking.

He took another step.

Heard one tick.

He stepped down.

Tick!

He looked at his shoes. The loose shoelaces had plastic tips that slapped against the stairs every time he took a step.

Next time Zipper had to go outside in the middle of the night, Zack was definitely tying his shoes first!

They made it outside.

"Okay, boy."

Zack unclipped the leash and Zipper raced across the porch, down the wide center steps, and into the landscaped lawn, where he made a beeline for the nearest tree and raised his leg.

"Probably better if he did that at the curb, don't you think, lad?"

Zack didn't want to turn around, but he did.

A roly-poly man chomping a cigar stood near the theater's front door. He was accompanied by two giggly girls who sort of looked like Santa's elves at the mall, only naughtier—with short skirts, long legs, and jazzy Robin Hood hats.

"I'm joshing," the jolly man said, pulling the cigar stub out of his mouth so he could let loose with a rumbling belly laugh. "Welcome to the Hanging Hill Playhouse, Zack! Your dog may piddle wherever he pleases. After all, you are the demon slayer!"

Zack crept backward down the porch steps, careful not to trip on his loose shoelaces.

The jolly man and his bubbly-but-dead girlfriends drifted forward and Zack remembered what Mrs. McKenna had said during lunch: Justus Willowmeier III "was seldom seen without a cigar in his mouth and a pretty woman on each arm."

Zipper came running over to join Zack in a circular patch of grass at the front of the building. Dark clouds raced across the starry sky, blotting out a moon that was almost full.

"Enjoying your stay, Zack?" Mr. Willowmeier asked from his perch up on the porch. The two showgirls batted their spidery eyelashes and smiled at him with plump, painted lips. Zack figured their lipstick must have been ruby red, but in this light it looked jet-black.

"Having fun in my house, lad?" Willowmeier hooked his thumbs into his vest. Bounced up on his heels. Waited again for a reply.

Zack nodded. Oh, yeah. He was having a blast.

"Attaboy. We were all quite delighted to hear you had finally arrived!"

"You're our hero!" one of the girls cooed.

"Um, I think you have the wrong guy."

"Nonsense. We have heard all about your courageous exploits, how you dealt with that nasty fellow at the crossroads. Sent him packing, eh?"

"Well, yeah . . . but . . ."

"Zachary," said Mr. Willowmeier. "I have a proposition to make. I would like to cast you in a leading role, here at my theater!"

"Why me?"

"You're special!"

"So's Meghan. She sees ghosts, too."

Mr. Willowmeier frowned for a second. "We know." Then he smiled and his face became a jolly pumpkin head again. "But, well, Miss McKenna's quite busy. The show must go on and all that. However, it may not go on at all if *you* do not do what needs to be done."

"Personally, we can't do much," squealed the other showgirl. "Except go to parties. Parties are fun."

"Thank you, Tina," Mr. Willowmeier said patiently. "Zack, here then is my predicament. My careless grandfather erected his tavern on top of what had previously been Hangman's Hill. Never a very bright idea, eh? But, let's be fair. He negotiated a marvelous deal on the land."

"It was dirt cheap," said the showgirl on his left. "On account of it being cursed by that Indian chief and all."

"Did the chief have a daughter?" Zack asked.

"Indeed," said Willowmeier. "Princess Nepauduckett. She was the first to climb up the Hanging Hill scaffold to the gallows. Back in 1639, I believe. Gross miscarriage of justice. Accused of crimes she did not commit. Corn thievery, which, I gather, was considered a capital offense in those days."

"She's still here," said Zack.

"We know. For years, we have lived here with her and . . . *the others*. Maintaining a fragile equilibrium. Now, however, some rather greedy mortals have arrived. They mean to upset that delicate balance and evict us from our home. That is why we are all so thrilled you're here, Demon Slayer!"

"Huzzah!" shouted a chorus of voices from somewhere up above.

Zack dared to look.

In the glowing windows of the second floor, he saw a whole gallery of ghosts. A chorus line of showgirls wearing colorful headdresses; two men in baggy striped pants, holding cream pies; a rotund woman in a Viking helmet, clutching a spear; a stagehand in a hat and suspenders, lighting sparklers and tossing them up to Juggler Girl, who stood balanced on one toe atop the tip of an ornate lightning rod, twirling the glittering fireworks in a dizzying circle above her head.

"Wow!" said Zack. "How many of you are there?"

"Quite a few!" said Mr. Willowmeier, rumbling up another belly laugh. "Anyone who ever traipsed across the boards or worked here behind the scenes, anyone who found their joy in the limelight, their happiness in the roar of the crowd, all are welcome to return!"

"Be not afraid of greatness, lad!" The swashbuckling Shakespearean actor Zack and Meghan had seen in the basement pounced to the ground in front of Zack, sheathed his sword, and propped his fists heroically against his hips. "Remember: 'Some are born great, some achieve greatness, and some have greatness thrust upon 'em'"

"Zack," said Mr. Willowmeir, "allow me to introduce Bartholomew Buckingham. One of the finest thespians it was ever my pleasure to know!"

"What say you, Zachary?" Buckingham asked, his vowels round and rich. He cocked up a single eyebrow. "Will you assist us?"

"Me? What can I do?"

"Much. For you are the demon slayer, are you not?"

"Right," mumbled Zack. "I'm special."

"Huzzah!" shouted Buckingham.

"Huzzah!" echoed all the others.

Zack wasn't sure, but he might've just said yes without even knowing he had said it.

"Oh, Zack?" said Mr. Willowmeier in a stage whisper.

"Yes, sir?"

"Not a word of this to Judy, Derek, or Meghan, eh?"

"How come?"

"I'm afraid they may soon need the protection of a demon slayer even more than we do!"

53

first thing Monday morning, Hakeem, Badir, and Jamal escorted Reginald Grimes back to the basement.

This time, they led him into the vast warehouse located two stories below the theater's scene shop. Hakeem flicked on a work light and Grimes was staring up at a brass statue of his new god.

"Is it the original?"

"No, oh Holy One. However, it is an exact replica. Handcrafted by our faithful artisans in Kairouan."

"Are they also my devoted followers?"

"But of course. They have provided much financial assistance for our endeavors."

Grimes stared at the metal beast. "The dog days are upon us, Hakeem!" he declared. "Sirius, the Dog Star, the brightest star in all the heavens, now rises and sets in sync with the sun. We enter a time of sweltering heat, when none will feel the hot blast from hell's furnace door as we pry it open. This is the evilest time of the rolling year, when the seas boil, wine turns sour, dogs grow mad, and mankind burns with fevers and frenzies!"

"You have studied well," said Hakeem.

"I took the book home last night. Reread a few chapters."

"Then you are ready!" Hakeem held up his key. "Let us go open the final drawer!"

The four men scurried across the basement to the room where the trunk was stored.

"It is time, Exalted One."

Hakeem's brass key glistened in the sharply angled beam of sunshine slicing through the casement windows.

The birds outside ceased chirping.

"It is time!"

He slowly inserted the key into the lock on the one drawer that remained sealed.

"Hurry up!" said Grimes. "Open it!"

"Guard the door," Hakeem commanded Badir and Jamal. "Let no infidels approach!"

They grunted. Went to the door.

Hakeem turned the key. The locked drawer clicked open.

"Show me!" said Grimes, quivering with anticipation.

Hakeem bowed, slid open the creaking drawer, and extracted a brittle parchment roll.

"What is it? Another ritual? More necro- or necyomancy?"

Hakeem grinned. "What if you could not only summon forth the spirits of the damned but restore them to full life?"

Grimes thought about that. "Bring the dead back to life? Resurrect them? Are such things possible?"

"Yes, Exalted One. Here, in this place, at this time, such things are very possible, indeed." He gestured toward the scroll. "Behold the resurrection ritual! Your grandfather, may Ba'al rest his soul, attempted to perform it. Once."

"When?"

"Many years ago."

"Where?"

"Here."

"Why here?"

"This building was erected on what some might call cursed land. What we would call sacred soil. It is a power spot. A vortex where negative energies collide. A swarming place for the foulest demons imaginable! It is land ripe for our resurrection ritual!"

Zack was eating Cheerios out of a paper bowl in Judy's room.

She went with the box of Frosted Mini-Wheats. They'd sliced up a banana and shared it, too. Zack figured he should probably be eating steak and eggs, biscuits and gravy. Something with tons of protein. Might bulk him up. Make him look more like what he imagined a demon slayer ought to look like. Like the superheroes in the comic books.

Zack had tossed and turned all night. Kept dreaming about show-people ghosts.

Not to mention demons in top hats toting bloody meat cleavers.

And Native American girls with bloated black tongues. And . . .

"How'd you sleep?" Judy asked.

"Not so good."

"Me neither. Lumpy pillow. Strange bed. Too quiet."

"Too quiet?"

"We've been living in that motel so long, I'm used to

my nightly traffic serenade. Tires humming. Brakes squeal-
ing. Eighteen-wheelers rumbling along the interstate at five
a.m. Last night, all I heard was quiet. And crickets."

Zack nodded.

Maybe the whole deal with Mr. Willowmeier and the
ghosts had been a dream. Either that or they had worked
up some kind of spell so nobody heard everybody shouting "Huzzah!" but him. Zachary Jennings.

Mr. Demon Slayer.

He needed another bowl of Cheerios. Maybe a multi-
vitamin with iron. Not to mention a sword or something.

"With this final ritual," Hakeem explained to Grimes, "you will assemble the ultimate cast! A living, breathing army of demons eager to do your bidding."

Grimes understood. "They could rob banks for me."

"Yes, Your Eminence."

"Steal gold. Jewelry. Stocks. Bonds. Anything. Everything!"

"Yes, Your Eminence."

Grimes felt the blood surging through his crippled arm. "A monster like Lilly Pruett could take revenge on all my enemies."

"And she will. She will do whatever you tell her to do. So will they all. They will be your puppets. You will be their puppet master."

"Show me what must be done."

"These are the words the male child must speak during the ceremonial offering."

Grimes moved to snatch the scroll out of Hakeem's hands.

"Careful! It is two thousand years old!"

"Then read it to me!"

"As you wish."

Carefully, very carefully, Hakeem unrolled the parchment and recited the ancient words. When he was finished, Grimes fully understood the magnitude of his destiny, the tremendous power he had been given.

The bloody deed that must be done to make it all so.

He was more than special.

He was very close to being a god.

His eyes grew wider and wilder.

"The boy must chant these words before the two children enter the holy place," said Hakeem. "Tonight. When the moon is full."

"Why these two children?"

"They were both born under a full moon."

"So that's why you got rid of Brad Doyle and hired Derek Stone."

"Indeed."

"Clever. And once Derek and Meghan have played their parts, once they make their 'exits,' I will become the undisputed ruler of all the reanimated demons we have summoned forth?"

Hakeem nodded.

"Good. Good."

"We, of course, hope you will see fit to share whatever riches you acquire with your loyal acolytes in the Brotherhood of Hannibal."

"Fear not," said Grimes. "You people have proved faithful and true. I shall prove generous and munificent."

"Badir? Jamal?" Hakeem clapped his hands. "Take the trunk. Hide it where no heathen might stumble upon it."

"Yes, Hakeem!"

"Then finish your preparations! All must be in readiness by moonrise tonight!"

"Fear not," said Grimes. "I shall be ready! So shall the children!"

56

Derek Stone sat in the corridor outside his bedroom on the fifth floor, thumbing the remote for his radio-controlled monster truck, the only vehicle his mother had allowed him to bring on this stupid trip to Connecticut.

He zipped it up the carpeted hallway. Slammed it into a spinning U-turn. Sent it flying over a bump in the rug and watched it carom off the baseboards. It was totally awesome.

"Derek?"

His mother. Calling from her room. He sidewinded the monster truck—with anodized aluminum wheel hexes and slipper clutch—into a sliding skid near the elevator alcove. Parked it. Out of sight. Out of mind.

"Yes, Mommy?"

"Rehearsal starts at ten a.m."

"So?"

"You've got an hour!"

"I know."

She stuck her head out her door. Her hair was in all kinds of curlers. There was green goop on her face.

"Have you memorized your lines?"

Derek gestured toward the script sitting in his lap, where it did an excellent job of hiding the monster-truck remote. "I'm working on it."

"Out here?"

"I concentrate better in the hallway."

"Fine. I need to finish putting on my makeup." She slammed the door.

Derek chucked the script aside. Clutched the handgrip controller. Sent the monster truck zipping into an amazing one-eighty backward tailspin.

The elevator bell pinged. The cage door slid open.

"Hello, Derek."

It was the director. Reginald Grimes.

Derek popped up. Waved. He was still holding the pistol grip controller in his hand.

"Working on your script?"

"Yes, sir."

"Good. Excellent." Grimes walked up the hall. He had a slippery, loping kind of gait. Looked like a camel with a mustache.

"First of all, Derek, let me say how thrilled I am to have you in my cast. You were always my first choice for the role of Charlie."

"Really? What about Brad Doyle?"

"Bah!" Grimes waved one arm dismissively. His other arm remained locked and frozen at his side. "Brad Doyle! That boy couldn't act his way out of a paper bag."

Derek smiled. It felt like it was his birthday. Maybe Christmas. "So you wanted me? Really?"

"Really! In fact, I don't want to overburden your artistic talents, but . . ."

Derek stiffened his spine. "What is it, Mr. Grimes?"

"Well, I am considering expanding your role."

"Really? Wow!"

"Yes. I'd like to attempt an artistic experiment. Make the part of Charlie a bit more dynamic. A bit more interesting."

"Awesome, sir!"

"Of course, no one must know about this. As I said, it's all very experimental. Very avant-garde."

Derek had no idea what "avant-garde" meant but it sounded better than his mother's constant reminders that he was a lousy actor, that he only got by on his dimples.

"I'm all about avant-garde, sir."

"Excellent. Wonderful." Grimes reached into a pocket with his good hand and pulled out a folded piece of paper. "You're not to show this to anyone. Not your mother. Not Miss McKenna. Not the Jennings boy."

"Of course not."

"It's in Latin."

"Okay."

"I spelled it out phonetically for you."

"Thank you, sir. That was very kind of you."

"Commit these new lines to memory before sundown."

"No problem, Mr. Grimes. I'm a very quick study."

"Excellent. See you at rehearsal."

"Ten o'clock, sir. I'll be there! And I'll memorize all these new lines, too!"

"Wonderful."

Wow.

This was it! His big break!

He really was a brilliant actor.

Reginald Grimes had said so!

Zack saw Meghan sitting on a sun-drenched bench in the lobby.

"Hey!" he said.

"Hi!" Meghan closed her script. "Do anything exciting last night?"

Zack shrugged. "Read a little. Watched an old movie on TV."

Chatted with Justus Willowmeier III, Bartholomew Buckingham, and a whole bunch of other dead people.

Zack wanted to tell Meghan all about the theatrical ghosts he had seen swarming outside the theater last night. But Mr. Willowmeier had specifically told him not to say a word to Judy, Meghan, or even Derek about what he had seen and heard.

I'm afraid they may soon need the protection of a demon slayer even more than we do!

Why? Was there some sort of demonic conspiracy brewing against *Curiosity Cat*? Didn't demons have more important stuff to do than mess around with musicals?

"So what'd *you* do last night?" Zack asked.

"Homework. Studied my lines."

"Homework? In August?"

"The principal of my school doesn't believe in summer vacations."

"Your mom?"

"Yeah. So where's your stepmom?"

"She went upstairs to talk to Mr. Grimes."

"Oh," said Meghan, "I almost forgot! I figured out why that girl downstairs was crying!"

"Yeah?"

"I think her name is Princess Nepauduckett. There was this etching that looked just like her—the buckskin dress, the beads, the hairdo—in this obscure Native American history book my mom brought back from the library."

"Cool."

"Not really. It was an etching of her execution. They hanged her for stealing food from the first settlers. The Pilgrims."

Zack pretended to be surprised. "Really?"

"Yeah. Hey, I wonder if Princess Nepauduckett knows *your* Pilgrim Guy!"

"We'll have to ask her next time we see her."

"Yeah! We know where to find her. I figure she's stuck downstairs."

Zack wanted to say *No. She also rides the elevator. Especially real early in the morning.*

But he didn't.

Reginald Grimes sat behind the cluttered desk in his office on the second floor, staring at the wall filled with framed posters from the many shows he had directed over the years: *Put On Your Shoes; My Gal Sal; Sing, Sing, Sing.*

All had received rave reviews.

All had brought him glory.

But none of those triumphs could compare with the glory awaiting him when the full August moon rose in the east and he, the anointed one, performed the sacred resurrection rite with the two children.

His worldly cares and concerns, his fears and his hates, his loneliness and isolation, all of it was fading away now.

He reached into a desk drawer and found the special hat Hakeem had given him to wear in his role as high priest. A purple turban with a luminous emerald clasp at its center. Just like his grandfather's. He placed it on his head. Felt its plump lushness.

There was a knock at the door.

"Mr. Grimes?"

It was Judy Magruder Jennings. The author.

"Yes?"

She was staring at his hat.

"Is that a costume piece?"

"Yes."

"For *Curiosity Cat*?"

"No."

"Good. Because none of my characters is a genie."

Grimes assumed that the woman was attempting to be funny.

"Is there something I can help you with, Ms. Jennings?"

"Yes. I wanted to talk to you before rehearsal. I don't think the lyrics should be changed."

"I see."

"So I'm not going to change them."

"Fine."

"Fine?"

"It was simply a suggestion."

"Oh. Okay. Thanks."

"Is that all?"

"Yep. See you at rehearsal. Ten a.m., right?"

Grimes nodded slowly. He wasn't even there. Wasn't really listening. The woman's words sounded like the *wah-wah* blaring from the bell of a muted trombone. Reginald Grimes cared nothing for *Curiosity Cat* or the Pandemonium Players or the playwright currently darkening his doorway.

He was the exalted one, the high priest of Ba'al Hammon—the voracious creator, king of the two regions, and ruler of the underworld!

Before anyone else arrived, while his mom was upstairs slathering on her last layer of face paint, Derek Stone had rehearsal room A all to himself.

He pulled out the secret script the director had just given him.

He stared at the paper.

Uh-oh.

The words were gobbledygook. Thank goodness for Mr. Grimes's phonetic translations!

"O, *magnus Molochus.*"

What could it mean?

"*Nos duo vitam nostram damus ut vos omnes qui huc arcessiti estis vivatis.*"

Okay. Something about noses and dames, which was what they used to call girls in black-and-white movies.

The door swung open. Tomasino Carrozza came bounding into the room.

Derek hid the secret script in his pants.

He'd have to work on this later. No more monster truck. No more Burnout Dominator on his PlayStation

Portable. No more goofing off with Meghan and Zack down in the basement.

Derek Stone had work to do!

Reginald Grimes thought he was a great actor.

He had lots and lots and *lots* of work to do.

"Sorry if the room's kind of messy," the company manager said to the group of actors gathered around the snack table at the back of the rehearsal room. "Mr. Kimble, our custodian, didn't show up for work today. First time that's happened since forever."

"You want a doughnut?" Judy asked Zack.

"No thanks."

She looked at him. "You feeling okay, hon?"

"Never better."

Zack wished he could tell Judy about all he had seen last night, because he and Judy had slain the demon of the crossroads *together*. Now, however, Mr. Willowmeier wanted Zack to fly solo. Why? Who knew? In Zack's experience, ghosts had their own screwy reasons for doing what they did, even if it made very little sense to people on the other side of the dirt. It was what made phantoms so unfathomable.

He just wished one of the night fliers would drop by during the day and give him a solid hint about what it was he was actually supposed to do.

"This is so exciting!" said Judy, looking around the room. "Our first real rehearsal!"

"Yeah. Maybe I will grab a doughnut."

"Okay. Then come sit next to me at my table, okay?"

"Okay."

Judy went to greet her composer, who was spreading out sheet music on the piano.

"Five hundred people auditioned for my part," Zack heard one of the actors say. "I was honored to be chosen."

"Especially by Reginald Grimes!" gushed an actress. "I heard he saw a *thousand* women for my role."

Zack wondered if anybody else had "auditioned" for his role as demon slayer. If so, maybe his understudy could go on, because Zack wasn't sure he wanted to do whatever it was Justus Willowmeier III and the other dearly departed show people wanted him to do.

He didn't want to keep dealing with the demands of the dead. In fact, he wanted dead people to leave him alone. He wanted to be an ordinary kid!

Of course, Zack still wasn't 100-percent convinced that he had seen what he thought he had seen last night. It might've been an incredibly bad dream.

Maybe he and Zipper had never even left his bed or seen Princess Nepauduckett dangling in the elevator or met all those other ghosts outside.

But what if it *was* true?

What if Meghan, Derek, and Judy needed him to be a demon slayer—just like Mr. Willowmeier had said they did?

Zack grabbed two doughnuts.

Reginald Grimes swept into the rehearsal room, followed by his assistant, Hakeem.

"People?" said Hakeem, clapping his hands. "We have much work to do today. Where's Miss McKenna?"

On cue, Meghan bolted through the door, followed by her mom.

"Sorry. I have a slight problem with the snooze function on alarm clocks."

"Deal with it!" snapped Grimes as he glowered at Mrs. McKenna. "Who, pray tell, are you?"

"I'm Meghan's mom."

"Why are you here?"

"Uh," said Meghan, "she's my mom?"

The door flew open again and Mrs. Stone stumbled into the room, teetering on six-inch high heels.

"Good morning!" When she flashed her glossy smile, Zack saw lipstick on her beaver-sized teeth.

"And who are *you*?" demanded Grimes.

"That's *my* mom, sir!" said Derek.

Mrs. Stone toddled forward. "Pleased to meet you, Mr. Grimes!"

He ignored her and slumped down into his metal folding chair.

"Announcement!" said Grimes. "Tonight, I'm hosting a small private party to honor our two youngest stars—Meghan McKenna and Derek Stone!"

"Sounds like fun!" said Derek.

"Oh, it will be," said Grimes. "I promise. Only the children are invited. Let's meet at seven p.m. out in the lower lobby."

"Where's the party?" asked Mrs. Stone.

"Downstairs. We've set up a room."

"In the basement?" Mrs. Stone sounded skeptical.

"It's cool down there!" said Derek.

Grimes smiled. "This party is really for the children, Mrs. Stone. Ice cream and cake. Pizza. That sort of thing."

"But we can come, too?"

Grimes hesitated, then smiled. "Of course. We look forward to the pleasure of your company. And now, will all those not directly involved with *Curiosity Cat* please leave the room?"

"Excuse me?" said Mrs. Stone.

"This is a closed rehearsal!" announced Hakeem. "Anyone not in the cast or in the crew must vacate this room. Immediately!"

Judy turned to Zack. "I could skip this first rehearsal."

"No way," said Zack. "This is the whole reason we're here. Zipper and I will be fine. We'll probably just hang out upstairs."

"You sure, Zack?"

"I'm heading over to the library," said Mrs. McKenna. "You're welcome to join me there, Zack."

"Thanks."

"Mrs. Jennings?" Grimes said crossly. "Are we ready to proceed?"

"I guess."

"See ya later, Mom."

Then Zack, Mrs. McKenna, and Mrs. Stone hurried out the door.

"I have never been thrown out of a rehearsal in my life!" fumed Mrs. Stone.

"My first time, too," said Zack. They were standing in the lower lobby outside the closed doors to rehearsal room A.

"Would you like to join me at the library?" Mrs. McKenna asked Mrs. Stone.

"Why?"

"You might find a book."

"And?"

"Right. Okay. See you back here at seven."

That got Mrs. Stone's motor running. "I don't have a thing to wear!" She clicked away on her high heels.

"How about you, Zack? Want to hit the library?"

"Maybe later. I need to take Zipper out for a walk."

"Okay. Do you know where the library is?"

Zack nodded even though he had no idea where it was located.

He nodded because the ghost of Bartholomew

Buckingham had just materialized over Mrs. McKenna's left shoulder.

"What ho, Demon Slayer!"

Apparently, it hadn't been a nightmare.

Zack waited for Mrs. McKenna to head up the curving stairway to the main lobby.

She, being an adult who wasn't Judy, hadn't seen or heard the swaggering ghost, his lantern jaw set on "heroic," his hands firmly planted at his hips.

"Uh, I gotta go." Zack bolted for the door they had used yesterday to head down the spiral staircase and explore the basement.

He slammed it behind him.

"What ho, Zachary!"

Buckingham was waiting for him on the other side.

"My, but thou art a nimble-footed knave!" He dipped into a bow that involved a lot of hand flourishes in front of his face. "I am your hoped-for guide spirit, here to assist you."

"What?"

"Did you not recently wish that one of the night fliers would drop by during the day to give you a solid hint about what it is you are actually supposed to do?"

Busted.

"Yeah. So, what am I supposed to do?"

Buckingham struck his hands-on-hips pose again. "Why, slay the demons."

"Right. But how?"

"That I cannot say."

"Why not?"

"Rules. Regulations. Those of us who tarry amidst the earthly ether are prohibited from directly interfering with mortal life."

"Listen, Mr. Buckingham, you've got the wrong guy."

That puzzled him. "You are Zachary Jennings, are you not?"

"Yeah, but . . ."

"You are the hero of the crossroads, is this not also true?"

"Kind of . . ."

"You, bonny lad, are special."

"Hey, I never asked to be special, okay?"

Buckingham nodded knowingly. "And I never asked to be ruggedly handsome, but, alas, as you can plainly see, I am."

"Look, I'm just a kid."

"Tut-tut. We have no time for modesty. In fact we have very little time for anything! You have less than nine hours."

"What? There's a time limit?"

"Indeed. Now then, I am not allowed to tell you all that I know." Buckingham leaned in to whisper. "However, my spies report seeing two burly ruffians secreting a theatrical trunk deep within the bowels of this basement."

"The what?"

"Sorry. The innermost recesses of the theater's subterranean maze of storage rooms and hidden tunnels."

"I really think you people should find someone else."

"Fie upon it! Screw your courage to the sticking place, Zachary! We need you. Meghan needs you. Derek and Judy, too."

"Are they in trouble?"

"I am not at liberty to divulge—"

"Are they in trouble?"

Buckingham first looked around to see if anyone was listening. Then he nodded frantically and mouthed a silent *Yes!*

"What kind of trouble?"

"The worst sort! Find the trunk, Zack! And beware Pandemonium!"

"Why do people keep saying that?"

"What?"

" 'Beware Pandemonium.' "

"Good question. I, forsooth, can not answer it."

"Fine. Then I'll just have to find out for myself."

"Huzzah! That's the spirit, lad!"

For the second time in one day, Zack realized he had accidentally said yes to something he really didn't want to do.

Reginald Grimes sat at the head table in the rehearsal room, pretending to listen to the actors reading their parts out loud.

He would probably give up show business when he became a billionaire. He wouldn't have time to direct vain and immature actors. He would have a multinational empire to rule. An army of demonic mercenaries to command.

"There will never be another cat like that!"

He looked up.

Meghan McKenna and Derek Stone were reading the scene that led up to the song about the missing cat.

"No, sir. Not in a million years!"

Jinx.

Grimes wondered if he could add a feline name to the list of souls to be resurrected.

Jinx might like to sit on his lap purring contentedly while he, Reginald Grimes, sat on his throne ruling the world!

It was only eleven a.m. but Zack was already exhausted.

He sat on the top step of the spiral staircase and gazed down into the basement below.

Okay. He had to figure out this "Beware Pandemonium" thing. Buckingham had just said it. The janitor had said it yesterday.

Zack knew that the Pandemonium Players was the name of the theater's resident acting company, but why should he be afraid of *them*?

He felt a chilling breeze drift up the corkscrewing metal steps. He leaned forward and saw yet another ghost materialize—a woman with wildly curly hair. She wafted away from the staircase and weaved a fluid path across the clutter of props and boxes stored underneath the main stage.

Wait a second.

Zack had seen the back of this particular specter before.

In North Chester!

Sitting in the breakfast room of the Marriott extended-stay hotel across from a guy sizzling in an electric chair.

It was Doll Face!

Mad Dog Murphy's girlfriend.

Zack clanked down the circular staircase as fast as he could to find out what the heck *she* was doing here.

Zipper was dreaming about squirrels again.

He liked the pillows on the bed at this new place. Nice and lumpy, squishy and mushy. He felt like he was in heaven, sleeping on top of a giant fleecy squeeze toy stuffed with Snausages.

And the sun hit these particular pillows perfectly! In fact, he was currently nestled in the most exquisite patch of sunshine and warmth. He figured that it was probably what lying on a beach blanket was all about for humans. He'd seen stuff on TV. Commercials for a place called Florida.

Zipper was in a happy, happy sunshine state.

Until something blocked the sunbeam streaming through the room's dormer window.

Probably one of those puffy white things up in the sky. Yesterday, Zipper had seen one that reminded him of a poodle. Another one sort of looked like Spencer, a golden retriever he knew.

Slightly chilled, Zipper stood up. Stretched. Yawned and dipped into a back-bending arch. Then he turned around in a circle, trying to find that perfect sun spot he had just been snoozing in. Couldn't find it, couldn't find it. So he changed directions. Circled back the other way. Still couldn't find it, still couldn't . . .

He heard a hiss outside the window.

He cocked an ear. Looked. Sniffed.

Yep.

There was a cat out there. On the windowsill. Gray and sleek with yellow eyes.

Zipper wagged his tail.

He didn't mind cats. They were fine—just, you know, *different*. Slept a lot. Tossed their own toys. Played with tin foil. Didn't know how to sit *or* stay. Pooped in a box.

But basically, cats were okay.

So he wagged his tail to let the gray cat out on the window ledge know he was happy to say howdy.

The cat shot out its claws. Yowled. Swiped at the window—scratching the glass.

Okay. Maybe this was a different kind of cat. A breed Zipper had never encountered.

For one thing, it was huge. Nearly the size of that raccoon he chased up a tree one time. For another, it looked sort of psychotic. Eyes all buggy and bulgy. Like Chico, this crazy Chihuahua who used to yap-yap-yap at him all the time when he was a puppy living in a kennel at Dr. Freed's animal hospital.

The cat hissed again. Furious and vicious.

Its eyes were glowing like the yellow warning lights

Zipper had seen on the highway. Foam drooled out of its wide-open mouth. Saliva dripped off its fangs.

As the hackles rose on his back, Zipper figured that this feline visitor was a few rabies shots short of a complete checkup.

He was just about to bark when the cat vanished. Disappeared!

Just like those ghosts back at the crossroads.

Which was fine by Zipper.

The fat cat had been the one blotting out the sun.

The pillow was perfect again. Like warm mud in July.

He needed a nap.

He yawned.

Snuggled into position.

Dreamed about squirrels. The slow ones—loaded down with acorns—the ones that were easy to catch.

Zack followed the curly-haired lady through the storage area under the stage, down the hallway on the left, through an open double door, and into a dimly lit passageway.

"Excuse me?" he cried out. "What are you doing here? Did you follow me? Why aren't you back in North Chester?"

Doll Face stopped moving forward. Drifted in place. Her clothes—a simple robe of some sort—and her tangle of coiled hair bobbed up and down as if she were underwater.

"Beware Pandemonium," the woman whispered, without turning around.

Her, too?

Zack felt fear crawl across his skin, then drop a bucket of ice down his spine. The lady's voice sounded strangely familiar. Did Zack know her? Doubtful. He didn't know many dead people, especially ones who hung around with convicted killers from 1959.

The curly-haired woman drifted down another passageway.

"Were you the ghost Judy saw going out of my room? Why'd you follow us here? Did you knock that picture frame over on purpose?"

The woman froze again.

Zack knew that if she had knocked over the picture frame, she must've been really mad or really sad, because that was the only way ghosts could make physical objects move.

The woman resumed her forward drift.

Doll Face was one weird ghost. Unlike chatty old Bartholomew Buckingham or Justus Willowmeier III, she hardly said a word—just "Beware Pandemonium," and *everybody* seemed to be saying that lately.

Also, her clothes didn't seem very old. Her robe was the soft gray of dove wings but looked kind of modern, so whoever she was, or had been, she hadn't been dead very long. Either that, or heaven had shopping malls.

They made their way past some dusty scenery pieces.

Doll Face turned left, walked under a brick archway.

Zack followed, wondering why Mad Dog called her that, because he hadn't even *seen* her face yet.

There seemed to be a golden halo of light rimming her body now, which was a good thing—otherwise the hallway would be totally dark. The overhead light sockets were bulbless. Apparently, they were moving into a section of the basement where nobody ventured—not even the cranky janitor.

Suddenly, Doll Face ducked down and stepped over a

low cinder block wall, through a very narrow opening that led into some sort of dank crawl space.

The air here was damp, thick with the scent of mildew. The floor was dirt, maybe mud. Zack, who wasn't all that tall, had to walk hunched over to avoid scraping his head against the rough beams in the ceiling.

Doll Face leaned forward and floated.

"Are we still under the theater?" Zack asked. "I think I hear the river. Do you smell it?"

No answer.

Maybe ghosts couldn't smell.

Zack had a funny feeling he had been led down here for a reason, and maybe not a particularly nice one. Maybe this ghost was the demon sent to slay the demon slayer.

"You know what? I think it's time I headed back upstairs. My mom's probably wondering where I am."

Once more, Doll Face froze.

This time, however, she slowly raised her right arm and pointed at something on the ground directly in front of her.

Zack moved forward. The ghost's stiff finger seemed to glow and illuminated a shadowy rectangle near her feet.

A steamer trunk.

An old-fashioned footlocker about four feet long with riveted ribbons along all its edges. Two hinged hasps flanked a lock that was already flipped up and open.

Aha! Doll Face had switched teams and was now

working with Bartholomew Buckingham, whose spies had reported seeing two burly hooligans hiding a theatrical trunk.

Zack read what was stenciled in faded paint above the lock clasp: *Professor Nicholas Nicodemus.*

Suddenly, the crawl space went dark.

Doll Face had disappeared, taking her glowing light with her.

68

"Hello? Hello?"

Yep. Doll Face was definitely gone. Zack was alone. In the dark.

Never his favorite place to be.

It was where he saw her sometimes.

His dead mother.

She was gone and buried, but in the dark, when he was alone with nothing but his feelings of guilt, scary memories, and wild imagination, Zack sometimes heard her.

"You're the reason I had to die! I had to get away from you!"

"It's not true!" Zack yelled. His voice echoed off the low ceiling. "I. Did. Not. Kill. You!"

Finally. He had said it out loud. Okay, he had said it out loud in the dark in a crawl space but he had said it.

He did not kill his mother.

She caught cancer because she smoked too many cigarettes. She smoked too many cigarettes because she was miserable and sad, not because Zack was horrible and bad. She made her own choice. Zack did not make her make it.

Stumbling in the dark, Zack felt up and down the sides of the trunk until he found one of its leather handles and gave it a yank.

This was what Buckingham had wanted him to find.

Somehow, it would help him save Meghan, Derek, and Judy. That was what he was going to do. He wasn't going to sit in the dark being afraid.

"So quit bugging me, okay?" he yelled at the blackness, hoping his real mother would get the message: He was absolutely, totally, and completely finished feeling guilty about doing something he hadn't even done.

Zack dragged the steamer trunk out of the crawl space.

He bumped into a few support posts, tripped over a crusty pile of rubble, and fell backward into a mud puddle that left his butt feeling all kinds of squishy, but finally, he found the opening in the cinder block wall.

He heaved the antique case up and shoved it into the hallway.

More darkness.

Where was a glowing ghost when you needed one?

Zack pushed the trunk up the corridor, figuring it could bulldoze over anything blocking his path. He paused once to catch his breath and heard the skittering claws of what he hoped was just a rat.

Zack pushed faster and hoped he could outrace the rodent.

To the light up ahead!

It was faint and distant but it was, indeed, a light—glowing brightly just beyond the next brick archway.

70

Zack shoved the trunk into what looked like a costume storage room.

Rolling wardrobe racks jammed with clothes hanging in plastic bags ringed the floor. It looked sort of like a dry cleaning museum with a three-hundred-watt bulb burning in the ceiling.

And no rodents.

Zack saw a dressmaker's mannequin wearing the Curiosity Cat suit being constructed for Tomasino Carrozza. It looked like a scarecrow standing guard.

Or, since it was a cat costume, a scare-rat.

Perfect.

Zack propped the steamer trunk up on its end, unsnapped the heavy clasps, and pushed open the lid. The trunk had a hanging rack on one side and a stack of drawers on the other. It was the sort of luggage people in history books packed when they sailed across the ocean.

Everything inside the trunk was musty. Zack riffled through the clothes. A black topcoat with tails, black woolen pants, a yellowing tuxedo shirt, and a shimmering black robe lined with red silk. He also found, hanging in a bag at the far end of the rod, a purple turban with an emerald green Egyptain beetle brooch pinned to its center.

"Cool."

When he pulled out the turban to examine the jeweled scarab more closely, he saw a poster plastered to the back wall of the trunk: *Professor Nicholas Nicodemus. World-Renowned Sorcerer and Necromancer!*

Underneath the headline was an illustration depicting a snooty-looking man in topcoat and tails. His lacquered black hair glistened under the turban, and his arms were folded across his chest. He was wearing the costume inside the trunk!

Zack turned to the stack of drawers on the right and pulled open the biggest one, the one on the bottom.

It was filled with tubes of paper.

He pulled one out, unrolled it. It was a poster showing Professor Nicodemus staring at a human skull with hazy smoke swirling up out of its eye sockets. The curling wisps carried ghostly visions of floating dead people. Little red devils sat perched on the magician's shoulders, assisting him as, apparently, he summoned dead souls up from the underworld to join him onstage.

Must've been some act.

Zack pulled another poster out of the bottom drawer. This one was printed on rough paper the color of a grocery sack and filled with shouting type.

COMING!

PROFESSOR NICHOLAS NICODEMUS

THE WORLD-RENOWNED SORCERER AND NECROMANCER
APPEARING IN

"DO THE SPIRITS COME BACK?"

ORIGINAL AND MORE MARVELOUS ILLUSIONS
THAN EVER PERFORMED BY
THE ANCIENT EGYPTIANS, THE MYSTICAL PHOENICIANS,
OR THE NECROMANCERS OF INDIA

• • • • •

SEE THE DEAD RISE FROM THEIR TOMBS!

• • • • •

GAZE IN AWE AS SPIRITS SOAR
ACROSS THE STAGE AT HIS COMMAND!

• • • • •

SPEAK TO YOUR DECEASED FAMILY AND FRIENDS
AS PROFESSOR NICODEMUS
UNLEASHES THE FULL POWERS OF RESURRECTION!

At the bottom of the broadside, just under the prices and performance times, was printed the name of the theater where Professor Nicodemus was to appear.

JULY & AUGUST, 1939
THE HANGING HILL PLAYHOUSE—CHATHAM, CONNECTICUT
A PANDEMONIUM PRODUCTION

Pandemonium.
There was that word again.
Zack had to find a dictionary.
Or talk to Meghan.
After all, she knew what "vicariously" meant. Maybe "pandemonium" was one of her vocabulary words, too.

All around him, actors were acting, singing, and laughing but Reginald Grimes wasn't paying any attention.

It was nearly noon and he was thinking about his grandfather: Professor Nicholas Nicodemus. A brilliant man who had failed so miserably.

Hakeem had told him the story: how the great one had blundered when he'd attempted to throw open the doors to the underworld and had completed only half of the resurrection ritual before being hauled away by the authorities to live out the rest of his days in an insane asylum!

"From the top again?"

"Hmmm?"

"Would you like us to take it from the top again?" the composer asked from the piano bench.

"Yes. Again! From the top."

He'd work the cast hard today. Wear them out. Exhaust them with vocal gymnastics and grueling dance routines. He'd run this rehearsal like an aerobics class in a sauna! He'd tell Hakeem to turn off the air-conditioning, let the room fill with the unrelenting humidity of August's dog days. After six more hours of strenuous exercise, every bone-weary member of this cast and crew would be too exhausted to venture back to the theater tonight and interfere.

Meghan and Derek he would dismiss early, as there was no pressing need to fatigue or drain them. Besides, the boy needed time to work on his new lines.

It was Monday.

That meant the theater would be dark. There would be no performances of *Bats in Her Belfry.* No audience. No uninvited interlopers.

In just over seven hours, Reginald Grimes would succeed where his forefather had ultimately failed!

The music stopped. The singing ceased.

"Lunch break!" said the stage manager.

"What?" said Grimes, sounding half-asleep.

"Lunch break, sir. You said you wanted to take an hour break at noon?"

"I suppose I did. Meghan? Derek? You two are done for the day. Go work on your lines."

"Yes, sir!" said Derek.

"I will see you again at seven," said Grimes. "The rest of you, be back at one. We will begin to choreograph the dance numbers. Be sure to wear your gym clothes. I want to see you sweat!"

"That's one hour for lunch!" said the stage manager.

The cast and crew shuffled out of the rehearsal room.

"Hakeem?"

"Yes, Exalted One?"

"Turn off the AC!"

So far, Judy wasn't impressed with her brilliant director.

He didn't even pay attention during the read-through. Jeff Woodman, the actor playing the father, kept calling Curiosity Cat "Monstrosity Cat" and Grimes hadn't said a single word.

She approached the head table.

"Mr. Grimes?"

He didn't look up. He was still completely engrossed in that big leather book, the one with *Professor Nicholas Nicodemus* embossed in gold letters on the cover.

"So who's Professor Nicodemus?" she asked.

That got his attention.

He looked up. Stroked his mustache with a single finger.

"My grandfather. It was a stage name, of course. Professor Nicodemus was one of the greatest magicians who ever lived! He even performed here."

"When?"

"During vaudeville. Back in the 1930s."

"What's in the book?"

"Secrets. Illusions."

"I see."

"Enjoy your lunch, Mrs. Jennings."

His jet-black eyes went back to the onionskin pages of his blasted book. He tilted it up toward his chest so Judy couldn't read what was written inside.

Shaking her head, she left the rehearsal room and went into the lower lobby, where the rest of the cast and crew were milling about, making lunch plans.

Who was this Professor Nicodemus?

What had he really written in that leather-bound book that was so fascinating?

"Meghan?" she asked. "Do you know how to find the library?"

"Sure. It's two blocks west on Elm Street. My mom was going there this morning."

"Great. Maybe she can help me."

"Do what?"

"Some quick research."

"Cool. You want me to tell Zack where you went?"

"Thanks. Do you know how to find him?"

Meghan gestured toward the door that led into the basement. "I have a pretty good idea."

"I thought the janitor said downstairs was off-limits."

"He did. But, well, as you might've heard, the janitor didn't come to work today."

Judy smiled. "I see. Enjoy your afternoon off. Tell Zack I'll catch up with him around six. And, Meghan?"

"Yes?"

"Don't break anything down there."

73

Wilbur Kimble dragged himself across the closet floor.

He had been locked up in the dark for nearly a full day. He was thirsty. Starving. Too weak to even speak, let alone cry out for help.

The closet door was so warped it made a tight seal along the bottom edge where it met the concrete floor. No light seeped in under it and the key was still down the drain, where he had dropped it when the sizzling ghost in the electric chair had made him all kinds of jumpy.

Wilbur Kimble was trapped. There was no way out.

His jailor, the spook who called himself Mad Dog Murphy, had vanished, threatening, of course, to come back.

He leaned against the closet door, closed his eyes, and dreamed of Clara—the one ghost he wished *would* come visit him.

"O, *magnus Molochus.*"

Kimble almost had a heart attack! Someone was out in the basement reciting *the words*!

"*Nos duo vitam nostram damus ut vos omnes qui huc arcessiti estis vivatis.*"

This couldn't be happening! The words! Spoken once again by a young boy. That pampered Hollywood brat Derek Stone!

Kimble attempted to pound his fist against the door but he couldn't find the strength to lift his arm.

"Help." His cry came out as a scratchy peep while the boy, oblivious to Kimble's presence in the nearby closet, pressed on.

"*Puer et puella, puri et fideles, morimur ut vos resuscitet.*"

Puer et puella. Boy and girl.

Puri et fideles. Pure and true.

Kimble knew these words.

Could translate them from the Latin, because they were the very same words Professor Nicodemus had made him utter the day Clara died.

Now someone had brought the words back into the Hanging Hill Playhouse.

Kimble had failed. He hadn't scared anyone away.

The moon would be full tonight, and the children—a boy and a girl—would still be in the theater.

Soon they might never be able to leave!

74

Derek sneezed.

The dust in this basement was abominable; breathing was like inhaling a sack of airborne plaster particles. He was surrounded by all manner of dust-covered trunks and theatrical props: a barber pole; a papier-mâché crown; whiskey barrels; a couple of baskets; and a fake pig, a wax apple stuck in its mouth, sitting on a silver serving platter.

He sneezed again. Wiped his nose. Sneezed some more.

Derek knew he needed to stop doing that.

He needed to memorize the new script. Mr. Grimes believed in him. He couldn't let down the one person in the world who actually thought he might be good for something besides sitting on the couch eating Doritos!

He wiped at his watery eyes so he could read the script without the words looking all smudged.

"O, magnus Molochus!"

He heard someone clodhopping down the steel steps of the spiral staircase.

"Derek?"

It was Meghan!

"Are you down here?"

Quick! He had to hide the script. He couldn't let Meghan McKenna see it. He couldn't let anybody see it, because it was supposed to be a secret, and if he blew that secret, Mr. Grimes would be as disappointed in him as his mother always was.

He thought about the whiskey barrel. One of the baskets.

The pig!

He plucked out the apple, stuffed his folded piece of paper into the fake swine's snout, and crammed the apple back into place—stirring up another cloud of dust.

"Hey, Derek! Whatcha doin'?"

"Dothing," he said, sounding wheezy. The dust. There was so much down here. He was toast. Toast with a rash.

"Have you seen Zack?"

"Doe."

"Was that a no?"

Derek's chest rattled as he breathed in. "Yes."

"You sound horrible. You'd better go outside, grab some fresh air."

"O-tay."

Derek raced across the basement and hurried up the steps to the lower lobby. His lungs ached, his ears itched, and his tear ducts were spritzing like berserk squirt guns.

He was such a weepy, sneezy, wheezy mess, he forgot all about his secret script and the supersecret place where he had so cleverly hidden it.

Zack stood in front of a mirror in the wardrobe room and tried on the turban.

It looked pretty awesome.

"Zack?"

It was Meghan, calling from somewhere in the basement's tangled maze of corridors.

"Are you down here? Zack?"

"Over here! Costume room!"

A couple second later, Meghan found him. "Wow!" she said. "What's that?"

"This neat magician's costume I found in a trunk! Well, a ghost led me to it."

"Juggler Girl?"

"No. A new one." He decided to skip the bit about how Doll Face had followed him here from North Chester. "I found some cool posters, too."

"Awesome," said Meghan, moving in for a closer look.

"Oh, I almost forgot," said Zack. "What's 'pandemonium' mean?"

"Hunh?"

Zack picked up the poster and unfurled it. "This guy was called Professor Nicodemus and performed here in 1939."

"That would've been in the days of vaudeville!" said Meghan. "They always had magicians, singers, jugglers."

"Okay. But the poster says this particular magician's act was a 'Pandemonium Production.' When I first got here, the janitor told me to 'beware Pandemonium.'"

"That's because he's an old grouch who doesn't like kids or actors, so he doesn't like the Pandemonium Players."

"Okay, but why are they called that?"

Meghan shrugged. "I'm not exactly sure."

"What does the word 'pandemonium' mean?"

Meghan assumed her best spelling bee stance. "Pandemonium: A place or situation that is noisy and chaotic."

"Was vaudeville noisy and chaotic?"

"Probably. Most theater is."

"Could the word mean something else?"

"Maybe," said Meghan. "We could check a dictionary."

"Yeah."

"Not as much fun as exploring the basement."

"I know but . . ."

"Zack, I think the janitor told you to beware of pandemonium because janitors hate watching other people make a mess to eventually make something beautiful."

"I guess you're right," said Zack, even though he wondered why Bartholomew Buckingham and Doll Face had said the same thing.

"Besides, there are so many other mysteries we still need to unravel! Why was Juggler Girl in that movie? Who set up the projector? And what about that weird statue of the man with the head of a bull? Come on! I've got the afternoon off. Let's go see if Mr. Minotaur is still there!"

"Who?"

Meghan assumed her spelling bee pose again. "Minotaur: From Greek mythology. A monster with the body of a man and the head of a bull."

Zack and Meghan found their way back to the archway that had led them to the gigantic statue the first time.

"Look at those gloves on the wall!" said Meghan. "They all kind of point toward the Minotaur's lair!"

"Yeah," said Zack. "I've been thinking: The Minotaur is sort of like Sobek, the Egyptian god of the Nile. He had a man's body but a crocodile's head."

"Don't forget Sekhmet," said Meghan. "Body of a woman. Head of a lioness."

They both paused and stared at each other. Zack had never met anybody fascinated by the same sort of stuff that fascinated him. In fact, he was used to bullies beating him up during recess for even knowing goofy stuff like Sobek and Sekhmet.

They rounded another shadowy corner, went down that switchback ramp, and approached the sliding barn doors to the scenery warehouse.

The doors were locked. A heavy padlocked chain was looped through the handles.

"That's weird," said Zack. "It was wide open yesterday."

"Shhh!" said Meghan.

Then Zack heard it, too: muffled sounds coming from the other side of the door. Metal hitting metal. It sounded like someone banging a refrigerator with a sledgehammer.

Meghan held her finger up to her lips, leaned in, and cupped her left ear against the steel door. Zack did the same.

They heard gruff voices.

"Hurry up, Jamal!" said one man. "All must be in readiness!"

"It will be!"

More hammering. Steel on steel.

"They must be building scenery," whispered Meghan.

"Yeah," Zack whispered back. "Or tearing it apart."

He felt a frigid breeze brush across the back of his neck. Goose pimples shivered down his spine all the way to his toes.

Judging from the expression on Meghan's face, her neck, spine, and toes had just hit the deep freeze, too.

They both turned around slowly.

Very, very slowly.

"Hello, children!"

They saw a shriveled hag holding a small hatchet.

The hatchet was dripping blood.

The *leering* crone was wearing an antique black dress with poofy sleeves and a high collar.

"So," she croaked. "You must be the two children! The chosen ones!"

Zack and Meghan shot each other a quick glance.

"Chosen for what?" asked Zack.

"To set us free!"

"Actually," said Meghan, "I'm just here to do a show. It's called *Curiosity Cat*. Oh, by the way, I'm Meghan McKenna. Who the heck are you?"

Zack couldn't believe how cool Meghan was, getting sassy with a ghost.

"Lilly Pruett!"

"Who?" said Meghan, totally unimpressed.

"Oh, I've heard what you children say about me while skipping rope." She swung her hatchet. Zack could see patches of dry blood on its dented blade. *"Lilly Pruett, said she didn't do it, she was lying and everybody knew it!"*

The hatchet was weeping blood now, splattering red

droplets against the walls as she swung it back and forth like a grisly pendulum.

Meghan and Zack weren't giggling anymore.

Lilly Pruett, however, was cackling.

"Lilly Pruett had six babies, chopped them up to make some gravy. When the kids were good and dead, she found their father and chopped off his head!"

Meghan looked at Zack.

Zack looked at Meghan.

They both yelled it at the same time: "Run!"

78

"Head for the door on the right!" Meghan shouted. "The staircase!"

They dashed across the cluttered storage space.

For some reason, this Lilly Pruett ghost seemed different from all the others Zack had ever met. More like a ghoul. The type that can actually feast on human flesh.

Zack sometimes wished he hadn't read so many books from the library's paranormal shelf.

"Lilly Pruett said she didn't do it."

Great. The hungry hellcat was right behind them.

"She was lying and everybody knew it."

"Hurry, Zack!" Meghan wrenched open the exit door and leapt into the stairwell.

"I'm coming!" Zack wormed his way around some Styrofoam headstones. He dared to look over his shoulder.

Lilly Pruett was right behind him, toilet breath steaming out her nostrils. She had her hatchet all lined up and aimed at his neck.

Suddenly, something grabbed hold of a belt loop on Zack's jeans and yanked him backward into the stairwell.

The door slammed, and on the other side, as he raced up the steps after Meghan, he heard a woman who wasn't Lilly Pruett scream, "Leave Zack alone, you crazy witch!"

He froze. So did Meghan.

"Zack? Who was that?"

"I don't know."

"She knew your name!"

"Yeah." He headed down the stairs. Went to the door.

"Zack? What're you doing?" For the first time since they'd met, Meghan McKenna sounded scared.

"I need to see who it was."

"Lilly Pruett might still be out there!"

"I don't hear her anymore." He reached for the doorknob.

"Zack? Be careful. I think she's different than the other ghosts. She might be able to actually hurt us."

"I know. But I have to see who just saved me."

Zack gripped the doorknob.

He squeaked open the door.

Peered into the basement.

"Lilly's gone."

"Good," said Meghan, coming down the stairs.

In the distant shadows, under the brick archway, Zack caught a glimpse of the curly-haired ghost—right before she vanished.

"It was her again," said Zack.

"Who?"

"The ghost who led me to the trunk."

"Who is she?"

"I don't know. I can never see her face!"

Zack felt a lump of guilt or shame or both jumbling up inside his throat. Sadness washed over him and left his limbs feeling weak. He felt like he had to cry, only he couldn't, because he didn't want Meghan McKenna to think he was a big fat baby.

A lone teardrop, the only one he couldn't control, streaked down his cheek.

"Sorry," he said.

"Don't worry," said Meghan as she rubbed the moist spot with her thumb. "We'll figure it out, Zack. I promise. Together, we'll figure it out."

"Oh, we have quite a collection of Hanging Hill theatrical memorabilia," said the librarian. "Especially for famous authors to look at!"

She led Judy and Mrs. McKenna into the rare books room. "I've pulled out all our historical playbills as well as the archives of our local newspaper."

"Thank you," said Judy as she and Mrs. McKenna sat down at a long table. "You sure you don't mind helping me look into this, Mary?"

"Are you kidding? I was a history major. I love this stuff!"

They flicked on two green-shaded lamps and went to work.

"Here's something," said Judy, coming upon an antique playbill. "Professor Nicodemus performed here in August 1939."

"Great," said Mrs. McKenna. "I'll check the local newspaper. See if there's a review or a write-up." She flipped

through the long sheets of newsprint in a book of news-
papers from 1939. "Here we go!"

Judy peered over her shoulder to read the article.

Nicodemus Packs Them In With
Mesmerizing But Horrifying Magic

Professor Nicholas Nicodemus proclaims himself a "resurrectionist" and boldly states at the
beginning of his current show that he will raise
the dead.

At first, this seems like innocent flimflam, the
type of puffery often proclaimed by other magicians plying their trade on the vaudeville circuit.

But in his performance at Chatham's Hanging
Hill Playhouse, the self-proclaimed necromancer
(one who communes with the dead), who wears
a turban suggestive of the exotic East, was anything but innocent.

After some mildly amusing hypnotism and
mind reading antics with willing volunteers from
the audience, the "professor" proceeded to summon forth "those foul spirits who traipse between
this world and the next."

The spirits first summoned were harmless
enough: a skeleton playing a banjo, a green gob-
lin with a violin, and a waifish young woman
surrounded by a flock of fluttering doves.

It was in the second half of his act that
Nicodemus crossed the line from innocent

entertainer to treacherous sorcerer as he pretended to call forth the souls of Connecticut's most notorious criminals.

He summoned William Bampfield, a Pilgrim sent to the gallows in 1636 after he killed his wife and three young daughters. Next came the most egregious example of Professor Nicodemus's ill-considered conjuring, Lilly Pruett, the psychopath who terrorized Hartford in the late 1890s. She swooped across the stage, brandishing her bloody hatchet, the one made infamous in the jump rope rhyme "Lilly Pruett said she didn't do it."

It was at this point in the evening's proceedings that this reporter vacated the theater. I am pleased to report that I wasn't the only gentleman in attendance who chose to walk out on Professor Nicodemus's misguided shenanigans. Pretending to dabble in spirituality for the audience's amusement is one thing. Terrorizing your spectators with foul visitations from the lower depths is quite another!

This reviewer has no idea how the "necromancy" illusions were engineered and, frankly, has no desire to find out. It was, in my professional opinion, tasteless and tawdry gimcrackery of the worst sort!

"Wow," said Judy. "Sounds like Mr. Grimes's grandfather put on a pretty twisted show."

"Mr. Grimes's grandfather?" said Mrs. McKenna.

"Professor Nicodemus was his stage name."

"Wait a minute," said Mrs. McKenna. "I heard Grimes was an orphan."

"Really?"

"I asked about his crippled arm and the company manager told me Grimes injured it in an accident at an orphanage when he was very young."

"Okay," said Judy, sitting back from the table. "Guess you guys will have plenty to talk about at that party tonight."

Meghan and Zack, with Zipper on his leash, bounded down the steps of the Hanging Hill's front porch just as their mothers walked up the winding footpath from the street.

"Hey, Mom!" said Zack and Meghan at the same time.

The two mothers laughed.

"Where are you guys headed?" asked Judy.

"Taking Zipper for a walk," said Zack.

"Good idea. I have to head back inside for more rehearsal."

"I don't!" said Meghan.

"Lucky you," said Judy.

"Meghan?" Mrs. McKenna said.

"Yes, Mom?"

"Don't forget—we still have schoolwork to do."

"I know."

"And you have to dress for the party."

"Really?"

"He's your director, sweetie. I think a nice pair of pants and a clean shirt would be appropriate. Be back by two, okay?"

"Okay!"

Zack glanced at his watch. They had about an hour to figure out why the Pandemonium Players were called that and why ghosts were telling him to beware of pandemonium.

Zipper led the way as they strolled along the sidewalk and headed for the library.

"Your mom's pretty cool," said Zack.

"Yours, too," said Meghan.

"Yeah. I guess I got lucky the second time around."

"What do you mean?"

Zack figured he might as well go ahead and tell Meghan the truth. "My real mom never liked me."

"How come?"

Zack shrugged. "I dunno. She said I ruined her life."

"Really?"

"Yeah."

"Well, Judy's a great stepmom!"

"Yeah," said Zack, feeling weirdly guilty the instant he said it.

"They close at one?" said Meghan, sounding surprised as she read a sign in front of the Chatham Public Library.

"August hours," said a lady wearing red reading glasses and standing on the stoop outside the library's front doors. "No air-conditioning."

"We just want to look up one word," said Zack.

The lady, who was probably the librarian, started hyperventilating. "You're Meghan McKenna!"

"Yes, ma'am. I'm—"

"In town doing that new musical."

"Yes. It's called *Curiosity*—"

"*Cat!* I can't believe you're really you!"

Meghan shrugged. "I'm me, all right."

"Meghan McKenna!"

"Yep."

"I'm Doris Ann Norris. Town librarian. Is that your dog?"

"Well, actually . . ."

"Oh, where are my manners? Won't you children please come in?"

"I thought you were closed," said Zack.

"Not when a movie star needs a book!"

Meghan scooped up Zipper. "Is it okay if . . . ?"

"Of course. Come in! Come in!"

Zack followed Meghan and Zipper into the building.

The librarian peered at him over the tops of her half-moon spectacles. "Are you somebody, too?"

"No. Not really."

"He's Zack Jennings," said Meghan. "His stepmom is Judy Magruder Jennings."

The librarian gasped. "She was just here! Just a few minutes ago! Oh, my! Famous authors! Movie stars! What an exciting day this has turned out to be!"

And the librarian hadn't even been chased by a crazy lady swinging a bloody hatchet.

"Does the word 'pandemonium' mean anything besides, you know, the usual stuff?" Zack asked once Meghan had signed a few autographs for various members of the librarian's family.

"Oh, yes." She led them to a short bookcase filled with encyclopedias and pulled out the volume marked "M."

Zack had always thought it was spelled with a P.

"Here we go," said the librarian. "Are you familiar with John Milton?"

"Not really," said Zack.

"Milton was an English poet in the 1600s most famous for his epic *Paradise Lost*. In it, he called the capital city of Hell 'Pandemonium.' It's Greek for 'all demons.' In Book IV, all hell breaks loose—literally. The demons scatter across the earth, creating chaos. The city's name, therefore, has become synonymous with disorder."

"Beware Pandemonium," Zack mumbled.

"Indeed. If such a city truly existed, I certainly wouldn't want to live there *or* visit it!"

"Can I ask another question? Why is the resident acting company at the Hanging Hill Playhouse called the *Pandemonium* Players?"

81

The librarian escorted Meghan and Zack into the rare books room, where their mothers had just been.

"These are the playbills from every show presented at the Hanging Hill Playhouse over the past forty years. Maybe in one, we'll find a producer's note explaining the acting company's name choice." She gave Meghan the 1970s and Zack the 1980s. "I'll tackle the sixties myself. You two would find the hairstyles far too amusing."

For half an hour, Zipper snoozed under the table while the three of them flipped through magazine pages.

Zack worked through the shows done between 1980 and 1985. *Put On Your Shoes. County Fair! My Man Stan.* Still nothing about why they were called the Pandemonium Players.

He opened the program for a musical called *Flipperty Gibbet.* He scanned the title page and the cast list, then moved on to the cast biographies—short paragraphs of theatrical credits, tucked around yearbook-sized photographs of the actors in the show.

One of the photographs made Zack freeze.

An actress named Susan Potter.

"Here we go," chirped the librarian. "Found it. Nineteen sixty-nine. The world premiere of a rock opera called *Chaos City*. 'We've chosen to call ourselves the Pandemonium Players to celebrate the inspired chaos that guides all theatrical journeys.' "

She was beaming.

Meghan was smiling, glad they'd finally found Zack's answer.

Zack didn't say a word.

He just kept staring at the photograph of the actress named Susan Potter in a playbill from the summer of 1985.

"It's my mother," he said softly.

"Judy?" asked Meghan.

"No. My real mother."

Zack borrowed Meghan's cell phone so he could talk with his father.

"That's right," his dad said. "Before we met, your mother was an actress."

Zack, Zipper, and Meghan were sitting on a park bench in the small town square in front of the library.

"Did you know that she used to do shows at the Hanging Hill Playhouse?"

"No. She never talked about her acting career. Your mother's parents thought acting was a waste of her time and her expensive college education. They encouraged her to give it up, which she did, long before I met her."

"Well, she did like half a dozen shows with the Pandemonium Players. I'm surprised she never talked to you about it."

"Yeah," said his dad, sounding sad. "Me too."

Neither Zack nor his father said anything.

"Guess I'd better go," mumbled Meghan. "Schoolwork."

"Dad, I gotta run."

"Yeah," said his father. "So, hey, how are you and Judy making out over there?"

"Okay," said Zack.

"The plumbers came today. Put in new toilets at the house."

"I'll tell Judy."

"Is she there with you?"

"No. She's still in rehearsal."

"Tell her to call me before she goes to bed tonight, okay?"

"Sure."

"Hey, Zack?"

"Yeah?"

"I love you."

"I love you, too, Dad." He closed up the cell phone, handed it back to Meghan.

"Are you going to be okay?" she asked.

"Yeah."

"Kind of freaky, hunh? Finding out your mother had this whole secret life nobody knew about."

"Yeah. But you know what's even freakier?"

"What?"

"In that photograph, she was actually smiling."

"What's so freaky about that?"

Zack turned to face Meghan and raised his right hand to let her know that what he was about to tell her was the absolute truth: "I have never, ever seen my real mother smile in a photograph."

"Okay. But have you ever seen any pictures of your mom from before you were born?"

"Yeah. Just now."

"I mean besides the one in the program. Just her and your dad, maybe, before you came along?"

"Sure. Their wedding pictures. A couple snapshots in the photo album. Vacations and stuff."

"Was she smiling in those?"

Zack thought about it.

"No." Even in her wedding pictures, his real mom looked super-serious. "That's why it took me a while to recognize her in the playbill."

"See?" said Meghan.

"See what?"

"You didn't make her stop smiling, Zack. That was something she'd decided to do long before you came along. If your real mom wasn't happy, I don't think it was your fault."

Zack smiled. "Thanks, Meghan."

"I gotta go. Catch you later!"

Meghan took off running, headed for the theater.

A theater where Zack's real mother had once performed.

Zack's heart started pounding harder.

That meant she could come back!

"Anyone who ever traipsed across the boards or worked here behind the scenes" was welcome to return, according to Justus Willowmeier III.

Anyone.

Including Susan Potter.

83

During a short rehearsal break, Reginald Grimes huddled in a corner of the room with Hakeem.

They spoke in hushed, tense whispers.

"I've been thinking about tonight. What do we do about the mothers?"

"I have an idea," said Hakeem. "The stage will be empty tonight, yes?"

"Yes. It's Monday. We're dark. No performances at all."

"Good. We can hold them there."

"Where?"

"Do not worry," said Hakeem. "Jamal and Badir will handle it. But tell me: Who else is residing in the bedrooms upstairs besides the Stone and McKenna families?"

"The playwright and her son. The boy with the glasses."

Hakeem nodded thoughtfully. "Invite them to your party."

"Are you sure?"

"Yes. The playwright must be detained with the other women."

"And the boy?"

"He will be dealt with."

Zack and Zipper lay on top of his bed on the fifth floor.

Earlier Zack had gone by the rehearsal room and heard a man screaming, "Five, six, seven, eight," which was followed by a stampede of feet and pounding piano music. He didn't really understand why Judy, the playwright, had to attend a dance rehearsal. Maybe in case they decided to change the words from "Five, six, seven, eight" to "One, two, three, four."

Since Judy had been busy, Zack came upstairs and thought about eating.

He wasn't really hungry, so he'd thought about watching TV.

Then he thought about reading.

He'd thought about a lot of stuff and opted for lying on top of his bedspread with his good buddy Zipper for about four hours.

He had heard birds chirp, Zipper snore, and ancient beams creak as the sun heated and clouds cooled the building.

Zack had spent the final fifteen minutes of his four-hour funk rubbing Zipper's ears while staring across the room at the glassless frame holding the family portrait on top of his small dresser.

Zack, his dad, Zipper, and Judy.

His new mom.

Maybe that was why he was spending the whole afternoon hiding in his room: It was what he used to do a lot when his *real* mom was alive.

She'd scream and yell, tell him how he ruined her life, how he spoiled everything, how he was worthless, an embarrassment, and a total mistake. Zack would retreat to his bedroom, lock the door, and play with his G.I. Joes and action figures. He'd make up imaginary friends, create his own world. His pretend family could sometimes make up for his real one.

Now he was afraid his real mother could find him again.

Yes, she was dead. He knew that. He'd been at her funeral.

But . . .

Susan Potter could come back to the Hanging Hill Playhouse just like Bartholomew Buckingham and all the others. In fact, she could be here right now, hiding in the shadows, waiting to pounce. Maybe she'd toss him off to Lilly Pruett or give the old hag a hand with the hatchet. The ghost of Susan Potter would do whatever she could to make Zack pay for being a horrid little ingrate who loved his pretty new stepmother better than his angry old dead mother!

Zipper yawned, stretched into a stand, and marched up the bed to give Zack a sloppy smooch.

"What?"

Zipper smiled at him. Wagged his tail.

"What?"

Zipper jumped off the bed, found his grungy sponge ball.

"Oh. I see. You think I've spent enough time up here feeling sorry for myself? You'd rather go outside and play?"

Zipper's tail wagged faster.

"You're probably right. Besides, even if she is here, my mother can't hurt me anymore." He said it loudly enough for any invisible visitors to hear him without having to strain. "None of the ghosts can." He climbed off the bed. "They're ghosts. They can't do diddly except make spooky noises, rattle the furniture, and scare me into hurting myself!"

Zipper brought Zack the ball. Dropped it at his feet.

Zack figured he'd play with Zipper downstairs on the lawn for a little while and then meet Judy when the rehearsal broke up. He grabbed a bottle of water off the bedside table in case he or Zipper got thirsty, then picked up the squishy ball.

"What ho, Zipperus!" Zack said, putting on his best Mount Olympus voice. "Lo! See how the mighty demon slayer tears the sun from the sky and flings it at the moon!"

He tossed the sponge ball out the door. Zipper chased

it. Zack figured they could play fetch all the way down the hall and into the elevator. He stepped into the corridor. Zipper brought the ball back. Zack threw it down the hall. Zipper chased it.

"Bring me back the golden orb from Apollo's chariot, boy!"

"My brother," whispered someone behind Zack.

He whipped around.

Juggler Girl had materialized under the Exit sign at the far end of the hall.

Zipper saw Juggler Girl, too!

He dropped his saliva-soaked sponge ball on the carpet and stared hungrily at the shiny circus balls swirling above the little girl's head.

"Help Wilbur!" Juggler Girl said, and dropped her arms to her sides.

Five balls fell to the floor and bounced down the stairwell.

Zipper took off after them.

Early that evening, Doris Ann Norris was at home sitting in her comfiest chair, sipping ice-cold lemonade.

Her weary feet were up on an ottoman; her contented cat was snoozing in her lap.

It had been some day at the library! First the world-famous author Judy Magruder Jennings had dropped by. Then the movie star Meghan McKenna! And the boy with the adorable dog!

Quite a day. She'd been so busy, she still hadn't gotten around to reading the morning newspaper.

Putting aside her glass, she picked up the paper and flipped through the pages.

Nothing too interesting. Same old, same old. Even the funnies seemed dull.

Then again, she had been brushing elbows with celebrities all day. There wasn't much in this newspaper or any other that could wow her today.

Eventually, when she reached the pages near the back—the broadsheets cluttered with used car and muffler repair advertisements—she did stumble upon one story that caught her eye:

Magician Nicodemus
Suffers Heart Attack
After Slaying Visitor

Nicodemus. That was the name of the magician Mrs. Jennings and Mrs. McKenna had been researching!

Doris Ann Norris quickly scanned the accompanying block of copy. Apparently, the vaudevillian Artemus Grimes, whose stage name was "Professor Nicholas Nicodemus," was one hundred and five years old and had been a resident of a mental institution called the Riverstream Hospital for the Criminally Insane ever since he killed a six-year-old magician's assistant at the Hanging Hill Playhouse back in the 1930s. Before collapsing in his wheelchair from a fatal heart attack, the ancient magician had killed a young man named Habib Mzali, a visitor from Tunisia. The police had not recovered the murder weapon, apparently a knife.

Oh, my. She knew Mrs. Jennings and Mrs. McKenna would want to know about this so she found her sewing scissors and clipped the article out of the paper. She would take it to the theater. First thing tomorrow.

06

Derek Stone was starting to panic.

He was having trouble breathing and it had nothing to do with dust, dogs, dandelions, or dander.

He was stumbling around the piles of junk in the basement, trying to remember where he had hidden his secret script. They were supposed to meet outside the basement door for the party with the director in less than forty-five minutes.

Mr. Grimes had said he wanted this new scene memorized by tonight. His mother had said he needed to change clothes and put on his tuxedo, which she always insisted he pack, wherever they traveled, just in case somebody wanted to give him a key to their city or something.

It never happened. Nobody ever thought he was that good of an actor.

Except Mr. Grimes. He was the first person ever to believe in Derek.

Wait a second.

He *was* an actor!

He could fake it!

He could use his training in improvisation, all those Acting 101 classes he hated, where he had to pretend to be a strip of bacon sizzling in a frying pan or a pebble in somebody's shoe.

"Oh, magnifying Malarkey!" Yes. The first line went something like that. "Oh, magnificent Mucus!"

He could do this. He could pull it off. The words were such phonetic mumbo jumbo, who would even know if he was saying them correctly?

Derek was feeling good again. Confident.

He heard a noise in the stairwell. Someone was coming down the set of steps that led up to everybody's bedrooms. Fast!

Derek decided it was time for him to leave. He dashed over to the spiral staircase, grabbed hold of the banister, and raced up to the lower lobby as swiftly as he could— taking the steps two at a time.

07

Zipper chased the bouncing ghost balls into the basement.

Zack chased Zipper.

There had been five balls; now there was only one and it was sitting in front of a door with *Janitor Closet* stenciled on it.

When Zipper bit into the ball, it poofed into a hazy puff and disappeared. Zack laughed, because with wispy steam curling out both sides of his muzzle, Zipper looked like he'd just been caught smoking a cigar.

Zipper whimpered.

Zack went over to give him a reassuring head rub and maybe a splash of water to wash the taste of ectoplasm out of his mouth.

"Help. . . ."

Zipper cocked his head sideways, raised an ear.

"Did you hear that?" Zack asked his dog.

Zipper barked what had to be a "Yes!" and started scratching at the closet door.

"Help. . . ."

"It's coming from inside the closet!" Zack banged on the heavy steel door. "Hello?"

"Help. . . ."

"Somebody's in there, Zip!"

Zack grabbed the doorknob. It wouldn't turn. He yanked it. It wouldn't budge.

"Hang on! I'll run upstairs! Get somebody to help!"

"No. . . ."

"What?"

"No. . . ."

"I'm going upstairs. . . ."

"No. . . ."

Zack lay down on the floor, put his head near the crack under the door.

"Sir, I'm going upstairs to tell them that you're in trouble."

"Don't!" The voice sounded stronger. The man sounded old. Grouchy. "The children!" Okay, now he sounded like the grumpy old-fart janitor.

"Hello, Zack," said a soft female voice.

He turned around. It was the actress. Not the bowing one. The singing one from *Bats in Her Belfry*. Kathleen Williams. She looked like a lot of the 1950s-style ghosts Zack had met back in North Chester: she wore a jazzy hat and a dress that swung out like a flowery bell.

"Remember me?" she said.

"Um . . . I saw you do the matinee yesterday."

"Was I good?"

"Yes, ma'am."

"Well, I owe it all to you, Demon Slayer."

"Hunh?"

"I told Mr. Willowmeier all about you, Zack. Told him how you slay demons, because I was on the bus. The one you set free."

"You were?"

"Sure. After my smashing success on Broadway, I became a nightclub singer. Toured the country! I was riding on that Greyhound to my next gig when we had that dreadful accident."

"And you were stuck in North Chester?"

"That's right. Until you came along. I owe my triumphant return to the stage to you, Zack. I owe you big!"

"Thanks. But, right now, well—there's a man locked inside that closet."

"Where's the key?"

"I don't know!"

"Gosh. That's too bad. Of course, I can't tell you what to do. . . ."

"I know. The rules. But Mr. Kimble is in serious trouble!"

"You know, I remember this one time on Broadway, my dressing room door was locked and I couldn't find my key."

"Miss Williams, I'd love to hear the story but . . ."

"So, I used my hatpin. Just jiggled it in the keyhole till I hit the latch and popped open the lock. Of course, I'm not telling you what to do, Zack. You'll have to figure that out all by yourself." She winked.

Zack's eyes darted around the room.

He saw a Styrofoam head wearing an old-fashioned hat. There was a big honking hatpin holding it in place.

"Thanks!" Zack said to the ghost of Kathleen Williams, who, of course, had already vanished.

Zack pulled out the hatpin, hurried back to the door, and started working at the keyhole with his makeshift lock-picking tool. After a few jerks and wiggles, the pin caught hold of something metal. Zack levered it up and felt the pin press against the hidden lock latch.

The closet door popped open.

88

"Zack? We're invited to the party. Zack?"

Judy poked her head into her stepson's room. It was nearly six-thirty. Time to get ready for the party with Reginald Grimes.

But Zack wasn't in his room.

"Zipper?"

The dog was gone, too. Maybe Zack had taken Zipper out for another walk. Judy was worried about Zack. While she was in rehearsal, her husband, Zack's dad, had left a message on her voice mail. Something about Zack discovering that his mother had once been an actress at the Hanging Hill Playhouse.

Judy had heard how cruel the first Mrs. Jennings had been to her only son. She remembered how shy and withdrawn the boy had been when she'd first started dating his father.

She also knew something Zack's father didn't: His son saw ghosts. Not in the metaphorical sense, either. Zack really saw them. Judy was afraid he had run off someplace to hide from the mother who might be trying to haunt him.

She saw Derek Stone heading up the hall.

"Derek?"

For some reason, the boy was wearing a tuxedo.

"Hello, Mrs. Jennings."

"Derek, have you seen Zack?"

"Yes."

"Where?"

"Downstairs."

"Okay. Thanks."

Judy assumed Zack must've heard about the last-minute party invitation from the company manager or someone in the cast.

They'd meet up in the lower lobby.

Great.

Now all Judy had to do was find something decent to wear.

And figure out how to keep Susan Potter away from her son.

The janitor guzzled down all the water in that twenty-four-ounce sport bottle Zack had grabbed.

Rehydrated, he had the strength to ask Zack a question: "Where's the blond boy? Derek Stone?"

"I don't know," said Zack. "Probably getting ready for the big party."

"What big party?"

"With the director."

"Tonight?"

"Yeah."

The janitor rubbed his face. "Of course. The full moon! We don't have much time. Are they going to a restaurant?"

Zack shook his head. "No. Apparently, there's a banquet hall or something down in the basement. Maybe in that big storage room with the Minotaur statue."

"Minotaur?"

"You know—a man with the head of a bull?"

"Moloch!"

"No. We think it's a Minotaur. . . ."

"Moloch!"

Reginald Grimes stood in the center of the scenery storage room, staring up at the gleaming brass statue of Moloch.

Grimes was dressed in white tie and tails, a satin-lined cape, and a jeweled purple turban—a costume constructed to be an exact duplicate of his grandfather's. Hakeem stood beside him, decked out in elegant acolyte robes and his red felt hat. Badir and Jamal had installed a massive stove hood directly above the statue, as well as all the ductwork needed to vent the smoke of their sacrifice directly into the playhouse's chimney system.

"All is in readiness, Exalted High Priest of Ba'al," said Hakeem, scraping into a deep bow.

"Excellent," said Grimes. "Let us proceed upstairs to retrieve the children. You are prepared to deal with their mothers?"

"Yes, Exalted One. The playwright and her child as well."

"Excellent. Tell me, Hakeem: Where is this portal? This power spot you speak of? Where is it that I shall first welcome my army of demons?"

"Come. I will show you."

Hakeem led Grimes around the statue, where he saw four ragged posts, about eight feet apart, poking up through the concrete floor like pilings for a dock that had long since rotted away.

"Behold the original foundation for the scaffold on Hangman's Hill," said Hakeem. "Feel the floor."

Grimes touched the ground. It was hot and thrumming.

"This is the spot cursed by the Pequot chieftain Sassakus for what the white men did to his daughter, Princess Nepauduckett," said Hakeem. "The mighty chief decreed that when the full August moon, the Dog Moon, rose in the sky, so too, in this cursed spot, would the foulest dogs of the demon white race. The white man's prayers, begging for deliverance from evil, have kept this doorway sealed for centuries with only the most heinous souls being able to seep through its cracks—and then only with the assistance of a powerful necromancer, such as your grandfather."

"Or me!"

"Yes, Exalted One."

Grimes worked his hands together in anticipation. "And if I invoke the resurrection ritual of Moloch at the precise moment Sassakus's Dog Moon rules the night sky . . ."

"You shall unleash the hounds of hell! All the demons summoned to this place as well as those who gather here every August shall rise up from the dead, return to their bodies, and take on renewed life! You shall be crowned the King of Pandemonium."

Grimes felt his chest swelling with pride. Even his lame arm felt strong and rippling with purpose.

"You and the mighty Moloch," Hakeem went on, "shall rule the world from this sacred spot as we, the proud brothers of Hannibal, once ruled the world from our temple in Carthage. All shall tremble in fear before you and Moloch Almighty!"

Grimes's smile stretched across his face. He ruffled out his cape and swept around to the front of the statue, where he could already feel the heat radiating off the grill situated between the beast's knees. Badir and Jamal stoked the roiling inferno below the gridiron with shovelfuls of fresh coal.

"Is the Tophet ready?" Grimes cried out, using the Hebrew word he had learned from *The Book of Ba'al* for the place where the fires burned constantly, where children were sacrificed in the worship of Moloch.

"Yes, Exalted One!"

Despite the searing pain, Grimes forced both arms high above his head. The three Tunisian men dropped to their knees.

"Hear me, mighty Moloch!" Grimes proclaimed. "Soon shall I feed unto you two children in exchange for that which I desire!" He lowered his eyes and spoke to the floor. "Hear me, foul fiends trapped below. These children, pure and true, shall die in this fire so that Moloch might resurrect you!"

It was time to fetch the two children born under the full moon.

Time to slay Derek Stone and Meghan McKenna.

"You bring any food, boy?" the janitor asked Zack, sounding more like his old self.

"No. Just the water."

Kimble braced himself against the closet's doorjamb and tried to stand up. He didn't make it very far.

"Weak as a kitten," he muttered.

"Hang on," said Zack. "I'll try to find you something to eat out here with all the props and stuff. If not, I'll run upstairs to the rehearsal room. There's always food in there."

"Aya. Don't want to pass out. Too much to tell you."

"Come on, Zip. Find us some food! Anything!"

Zipper took off, sniffing at all the trunks, sticking his nose into a bunch of the baskets, snorting up a storm. Zack looked around the basement and saw all sorts of fake food. Plastic fruit. The Cratchit family's mammoth tom turkey—carved out of foam—from *A Christmas Carol*. On the rear wall, he saw all those gloves and gauntlets again plus a string of sausages. Wax sausages.

Zack looked again.

The gloves were no longer pointing to the right. All the fingers were aimed at the center of the room.

Zack turned around.

Now he noticed something else pretty peculiar: A quiver of arrows was pointing toward a spear, the tip of which was pointing toward a grandfather clock, the hands of which were pointing toward a parasol, the top of which was pointing to a stuffed pig on a platter.

Ghosts. They had their ways of dropping hints when they wanted to.

The pig looked like it was made out of plastic but the apple jammed in its snout looked pretty real. Zack plucked it out. Nope. More fake fruit.

But there was something hidden inside the pig. A folded sheet of paper. Zack pulled it out. Started reading it.

"Magnus Molochus . . ."

"Don't!" cried the janitor. "Don't!"

That was when Zipper barked.

"Find something, boy?"

Another bark.

"Hang on!"

Zipper was nosing outside the vents of a dented locker.

Zack opened the locker door. Inside, he saw some rolled-up blueprints, a rumpled coat, and a lunch bag.

"Score!"

Inside the bag was a moldy bologna sandwich in a plastic bag, Cheetos, Ho Hos, a Snickers bar, and a bottle of Snapple.

Zipper moaned like he wanted the bologna.

"Forget it," said Zack. "It's green." Zack hurried back

to the closet with the junk food that was so tightly sealed it had never gone bad.

"Here you go." He tore the wrapper off the Snickers bar and handed it to Kimble. The old man wolfed it down in four quick chomps. Revived, he glared hard at Zack.

"Those words . . . the ones you were just saying . . ."

" 'Magnus Molochus'?"

Kimble nodded.

"They were written on a sheet of paper I found."

Kimble gestured for Zack to hand him the paper.

"Do you read Latin, son?"

"No," said Zack. "But I don't think anybody does these days."

"Oh yes, they do," said Kimble. "The minions of Moloch. This is their resurrection ritual." Kimble handed the paper back to Zack and started reciting its verses from memory. " 'O, magnus Molochus.' That translates to 'O, mighty Moloch.' "

"Okay."

" 'Nos duo vitam nostram damus ut vos omnes qui huc arcessiti estis vivatis.' "

"What's that mean?"

"We two our lives do give so all you summoned here might live."

"Two people are giving up their lives?"

"Aya. That's how the ritual works. It's a swap, see? Two innocents for a legion of the damned."

Zack glanced at the script, read the next line out loud:

"'*Puer et puella, puri et fideles, morimur ut vos resuscitet.*'"

Kimble translated: "Boy and girl, pure and true, we die so that He might resurrect you."

"Wait a second. Is it Meghan and Derek?"

Kimble kept going from memory. "'*Animas nostras tradimus ut vestrae successus prosperos habeant.*' We give up our souls so yours will prosper well. '*In ignem ingredimur ut vos inferna fugiatis.*' We enter the fire so you can escape hell."

"Fire? Are Meghan and Derek going into some kind of fire?"

"Aya."

"This is crazy. You're telling me that somebody's going to try to kill Meghan and Derek, burn them alive, so they can get somebody else out of hell?"

"Everybody else. *All* the demons."

That hit Zack hard. "Pandemonium! When are they going to do this thing?"

"When the full moon rises."

"That's tonight! It was nearly full yesterday."

"When it rises, the ceremony will commence. Both your friends will be offered up as a sacrifice to Moloch."

"What?"

"They'll be roasted alive across the lap of that statue you say you found downstairs."

"The Minotaur!" said Zack. "How come you know all this?"

"Professor Nicodemus once made me recite those very same words."

"The magician?"

"Aya. Seventy years ago, he made me say them out loud. Then he threw my baby sister Clara into the fire! I helped him kill her!"

"You look very pretty!" Judy said to Meghan when she came into the lower lobby and joined the group clustered near the door to the basement.

"My mom said I should wear a dress."

"And I was right," said Mrs. McKenna. "Come on, a private party with the director is a big deal."

"I guess."

"Have you guys seen Zack?" Judy asked. "Derek said he saw him downstairs."

Derek blanched. "Not recently."

"What?"

"I meant I saw him down here earlier."

An elevator door slid open near the concession stand.

"Good evening, ladies and gentleman!" Grimes called out as he glided across the carpet, trailed by his assistant, Hakeem.

Judy, who had thrown on a clean white blouse and a fresh pair of jeans, felt seriously underdressed: Grimes had on white tie and tails, a cape, and a turban. Hakeem was decked out in some sort of religious-looking robe-and-fez combo.

"Excuse me," said Judy. "I need to run back upstairs. My stepson, Zack, is—"

"Already downstairs," said Grimes. "He was kind enough to come by early and help us blow up balloons. Shall we?" He gestured toward the elevator. "I thought we might go upstairs first, take a quick tour of Dracula's castle. You've seen the show?"

"Yes, sir," said Derek. "It's awesome!"

"Thank you."

"Sir?"

"Yes, Derek?"

"Were we supposed to wear costumes like you guys?"

"This?" The director laughed. "No. I'm going to perform a few of my grandfather's magic tricks at the party! Thought I should dress the part."

"Cool."

"But first, I want to take you folks backstage, give you a guided tour. Show you how we pull off some of the illusions."

He gestured toward the elevator.

They all stepped into the waiting car.

Hakeem pulled the accordion cage door shut. Pressed a button. The elevator rose.

"I wish Zack was here," said Judy. "He loves magic tricks."

"I gave your stepson a private tour earlier," said Grimes.

"Really? That was nice."

"I know."

267

Hakeem held out a cloth sack.

"Cell phones, pagers, and beeping watches, if you please," he said.

"Why?" asked Mrs. McKenna.

"I despise electronic interruptions," said Grimes. "Your valuables will, of course, be returned to you immediately after our little party."

Judy looked at Mary McKenna. They both shrugged. What the heck? They placed their cell phones into the sack. Meghan added hers. Derek tossed in his PlayStation Portable.

The elevator car stuttered to a stop.

The doors slid open.

Badir and Jamal were waiting on the other side.

They were both armed with pistols.

93

"I've had seventy years to think about what I said that night," Kimble mumbled. "I memorized those Latin words. Found a priest who translated 'em for me, taught me all about Moloch."

"Who is he?" Zack asked.

"Pagan god. Phoenicians worshipped him. Folks who lived in Carthage, what they call Tunisia these days." Kimble reached for the bottle of juice Zack had found in the lunch bag, and took a long swallow. "A lot of ancient civilizations used to practice child sacrifice. Aztecs. Incas. Carthaginians."

"And the parents let them do this?"

"Aya. In some cultures, the families had so many children they were willing to sacrifice one of it meant they'd receive some sort of special favor from the gods for all the rest. Good crop. Wealth and riches. New life for a bunch of dead criminals so you can send 'em out into the world to do your bidding. That's what Professor Nicodemus was up to."

"He was a necromancer," said Zack, remembering the poster.

"That's right. And he was the real deal. Could actually call forth the dead, have 'em float across the stage. I've seen it. Clara and I were on the same vaudeville bill with him."

"You saw him call up demons from the dead?"

"At every show. He knew all the ancient rites. Carried around this big leather book. *The Book of Ba'al.* He figured he could run the resurrection ritual and all of the demons would come back to life beholden to him."

He'd be the mayor of demon city, thought Zack. *Pandemonium.*

"Wish I'd known what he was making me say," Kimble continued. "Clara and I thought we were auditioning for roles as his juvenile assistants."

"He killed your sister? Burned her alive?"

"Aya. But, he forgot to vent his grill properly. Smoke billowed out all the windows. Fire trucks showed up. Police, too. I lived. Clara died. The professor was shipped off to the loony bin. The sacrifice was not completed. Moloch's promise remained unfulfilled."

"So you stayed here all these years to protect kids from falling into the same trap you and your sister did?"

"That's right. I never knew when the next descendant of the high priest of Ba'al might show up, try to kill another child like my sister, Baby Clara. The best juggler in all vaudeville."

"Juggler Girl!"

"What?"

"And your name's Wilbur! She sent Zipper and me

down to rescue you. Dropped one of her balls down the stairwell."

"When?"

"Just now."

"You saw Clara?"

"Sure. I've seen her a couple times."

Kimble's lips quivered. "How does she look?"

"Fine. Has on this frilly dress. Juggles all sorts of stuff. Balls. Bowling pins."

"Is she burned?"

"What?"

"Is she scarred from the fire?"

"No. Like I said, she looks fine."

"You promise?"

"Cross my heart!"

Kimble swiped his rough hand across his damp eyes. "What I wouldn't give to see her face again."

"Well, most adults can't see ghosts. . . ."

"It's because I killed her. That's why I could see that ugly ghost in the closet but not my baby sister!"

"No. It's just how it is. Besides, you didn't kill Clara. That psycho professor guy did."

"But it was my fault."

For a split second, Zack wondered if that was why he could see all sorts of spirits but not his own mother's!

Was it his fault she was dead?

"You'll see her," Zack said, trying to comfort the old man.

"When?"

Zack didn't know the answer to that one, so he made something up. "Just as soon as we stop these people from killing Meghan and Derek! Where's the nearest phone? We need to call the police!"

"Upstairs," said Kimble. "Stage manager's desk in the wings backstage."

"Let's go!"

Kimble hauled himself up off the floor. "We need to be careful, son. Moloch is mighty!"

Yeah. So Zack had heard. In the original Latin, too.

"This way, ladies!" snarled one of the thugs, waggling his pistol at the three mothers. "Into the vault!"

The other giant had his weapon trained on Meghan and Derek.

"What do you think you're doing?" Judy demanded.

The big man snorted a laugh. "Locking you three inside Dracula's tomb. Hurry up. It's nice 'n' cozy."

"Forget it," said Judy.

"Silence, infidel!" screamed Grimes. "Do not dare to interfere with my destiny! You are nothing! Nobody! I am the high priest of Ba'al Hammon!" He roughly grabbed hold of Meghan's shoulders. Hakeem snatched Derek.

"Mom?" Derek cried.

Mrs. Stone fainted and fell to the floor.

She wasn't going to be much help, Judy realized.

"Into the box!" The swarthy man jabbed the muzzle of his pistol into Judy's back.

"No!" said Meghan's mom. "Let go of my daughter!"

The other thug thumbed back the hammer on his revolver. Aimed it at Meghan's head. "Do what my friend Jamal says or I blow out this one's pretty little brains."

"Come on, Mary," said Judy. "They mean business."

"Indeed we do!" said Grimes. "Tie them up! Blindfold them! Put them inside Dracula's tomb!"

Ropes wrapped tight around her hands and ankles, a thick cloth covering her eyes, Judy was forced into the set piece that had been Dracula's sealed tomb in the show. She figured it was a version of a magician's substitution box, a classic magic trick she'd learned about while researching one of her books.

Judy heard Mrs. McKenna crying as she was shoved into the dark box.

"Grab hold of this other one's legs," snarled the thug named Jamal. "I'll take the arms."

Mrs. Stone's limp body was dumped between Judy and Mary McKenna.

Someone slammed the tomb door shut.

Judy heard heavy chains being wrapped around and around the box. Locks snapping into place. Yep. Just like in the magic trick.

Now she just hoped she could remember how the trick worked.

How the magician escaped!

Zipper watched the old man start climbing a ladder bolted to the basement wall.

"This'll be faster," the man said. "Take us straight up to the wings and the stage manager's desk."

"I'll be right back, Zip," Zack said as he grabbed a ladder rung.

Zipper knew Zack to be a boy of his word.

So he sank down on all fours. Panted a little.

He'd wait.

"Hurry!" Zack called out to the man climbing up the ladder ahead of him.

"Movin' as fast as I can."

"We need to move faster!"

Zipper barked. Zack was right. The old guy was slow.

He heard their feet *clunk-clunk-clunk*ing up the ladder.

Real slow.

Now he heard a hiss. He perked up his ears. Swung his head to the right.

His hackles shot up like porcupine quills.

The cat.

The crazy thing was back.

The goons named Badir and Jamal shoved Meghan and Derek down the switchback ramp leading to the storage room.

And the Minotaur, thought Meghan.

She could smell something burning. Oily. Foul. Like a malfunctioning furnace.

Mr. Grimes and Hakeem shoved open the swinging barn doors.

"Inside!" growled Badir.

Meghan felt the pistol muzzle being jabbed into her ribs. "Now!"

"Shall I lock the doors?" Hakeem asked.

"No need," Grimes chortled. "We're all alone. Leave them open wide so my army of demons can march forth to conquer the world!"

"What about the other boy?"

"The playwright's son? Bah! The child is a weakling! He is no match for Moloch and me!"

Meghan would've disagreed with the lunatic but she was too busy staring at the brass man-beast.

There was a barbeque grill between its knees and it was glowing, turning red like a burner on an electric stove top.

The bull's horns were acting like chimneys, sending streams of wavering heat and smoke straight up to the exhaust hood.

Grimes raised his arms toward the statue.

"King of the two regions, I invoke you!" he cried out.

Meghan stared toward the ceiling. She knew they were about two stories below the stage-right side of the theater. That was where the scene shop was—the place where they constructed all the set pieces for shows.

If this was a storage room for scenery, that meant there *had* to be some sort of freight elevator. A trapdoor. Some way to raise and lower heavy objects. Otherwise, how did they get the statue down here?

Now Hakeem, Grimes's assistant, stepped toward the statue. "Mighty Moloch, for lo these many years have we waited for this moment!"

Meghan looked over at Derek. He was trembling.

"We have longed for a high priest of Ba'al, an heir to the royal bloodline, to journey forth to this portal under the full dog moon to unleash our avenging army of demons!"

Okay. Now Meghan's knees were knocking, too. She'd met one demon—Lilly Pruett. But a whole army?

"Brotherhood of Hannibal, prepare to reap your reward!" cried Hakeem. "Prepare to raise a legion of merciless mercenaries to restore the glory that was Carthage! My brothers, prepare for Pandemonium!"

Meghan knew what that meant.

They were going to reestablish the capital city of Hell!

97

"There has to be a sliding panel!" said Judy.

"What?" said Meghan's mom.

Mrs. Stone didn't say anything. She was still passed out, squeezed in tight between Judy and Mrs. McKenna in the claustrophobic substitution box.

"That's how magicians do this trick! They slip off the ropes, then slide out the secret panel to switch places with their assistant."

"Where do they put the secret escape hatch?"

"Well, it can't be on the front or the two sides," said Judy. "The audience would see the magician sneaking out. So, it has to be on the bottom or the back. Feel around for it!"

They both slid down as far as they could with their hands tied behind their backs, their ankles bound. Judy patted her palms against the rear wall, then the floor, feeling for a hidden switch or lever. Being blindfolded didn't make the search any easier.

"We need to get out of here," said Mrs. McKenna, sounding frantic. "Those men have Meghan!"

"We'll find her. Derek, too. And Zack! Where's Zack?"

"With Wilbur," said a young girl.

Judy and Mrs. McKenna froze.

They couldn't see who the little girl was.

But they both heard what sounded like rubber balls bouncing around on the crate's wooden floor.

28

Mr. Kimble crawled through the trapdoor first.

"I'll go phone the police!" he shouted down the ladder to Zack. "Meet me at the stage manager's desk! It's behind the black curtains stage right!"

"Hurry!" said Zack. He hauled himself up the final four rungs of the ladder, came up through the trapdoor.

The curly-haired ghost was waiting for him.

"Hello, Zack."

He could finally see her face.

It looked just like it did in the theater program.

Young and happy.

His mother.

His real mother. Susan Potter. When she was in her twenties and her hair was wild and curly, not flat and straight like Zack remembered it. This was his mother before Zack had been born. Before she had even met his dad.

"It's so good to see you again. Let me look at you!"

Zack retreated two steps. Bumped up against some ropes and sandbags.

"W-w-what do you want?" he stammered.

"To help you! That's why I moved the gloves. To point the way to the statue! Then I led you to the trunk and protected you from Lilly Pruett and helped you find the hidden script. Don't you see, Zack? I want to help you and Judy."

"You leave Judy alone!"

"No, Zack. You don't understand. I'm trying to . . ."

"Shut up! I know what you're trying to do!"

For a moment, the ghost of his dead mother said nothing. Then she smiled. "You were always so different, Zack. So very special."

Was she mocking him?

"I think it's because you were born under a full moon."

Oh, yeah. She might be dead, but she was still the same.

"You should be downstairs, Zack. He can't complete the ritual without children born under a full moon."

So that was why she'd saved him from Lilly Pruett. She was making some kind of deal with Moloch. Offering Zack as another kid to be fed into the fire.

"You were spying on me at the hotel back in North Chester, weren't you?"

"No, Zack."

"You were there with that guy in the electric chair! He called you Doll Face."

"Yes, but . . ."

"Is Mad Dog Murphy one of your new pals?"

"No, Zack."

"Yeah, right. You broke the picture frame in my room, didn't you?"

"I'm sorry."

"You could only do that if you were really, really mad."

"Or happy."

"No, you're mad because I'm finally happy!"

Her terrifying smile broadened. "Are you, Zack?"

"Absolutely!" He spat the word at her. "Happier than I ever was with you!"

And then Zack figured it out.

"You hate that, don't you? You hate that I'm happy!"

"No, Zack."

"You're lying! I know what you're trying to do! You're trying to slow me down! You want Judy dead!"

"No, Zack. Listen . . ."

"Shut up, you wicked witch! I didn't kill you and I won't let *you* kill Judy or Meghan or even Derek!"

The ghost of his mother stopped smiling.

"I'm sorry, Zack."

"Why? Because I figured out your stupid plan?"

Susan Potter disappeared as quickly as the fog off a mirror when you throw open the bathroom door.

Hah! Got her!

One demon down, who knew how many more to go?

"Zack!" It was Mr. Kimble. Off in the shadows. "Help!"

The sleek gray cat was fast.

Very fast.

Zipper chased it up the spiral staircase.

Across the lower lobby.

Up the curving staircase.

Very, very fast.

Into the main lobby. Around the box office. Under the velvet ropes, over the stack of playbills, down the side of the lobby, through a door.

A closed door.

Zipper hit the brakes.

Smacked into the door.

He wasn't a ghost. Couldn't run through solid objects. The cat could. Cheater.

100

"Don't be afraid," said the soft, childish voice.

"Who are you?" Judy asked the darkness.

"Clara Kimble. Mr. Harry Houdini showed me how to do this trick, ages ago. Feel on the floor. Near your feet."

"I don't feel a thing," Mrs. McKenna grunted.

"Not you, silly. You!"

Judy felt a rush of cold air, as if she had just stuck her head inside the freezer case at the supermarket to check out the ice cream. She slid her feet around on the floor.

"Got it! Found it!"

"Great!" said Meghan's mom.

"Push it sideways," said the girl. "Push it now!"

Judy pushed. She heard a soft thunk. A panel flopped open under her feet and she tumbled out onto the floor.

"What about the rope? My hands?"

"Move the knots around," whispered the girl. "Find the slack. There is always slack. Houdini said so!"

Yes! Judy found the slack, wrestled her hands free, and pulled off her blindfold. Started to work on the ropes binding her ankles. "Thanks, Clara!"

Clara was gone.

"Hang on, Mary!" Judy crawled back into the box. Maneuvered around Derek's unconscious mom. Started untying Mrs. McKenna's wrists and ankles.

"Was that a ghost?" Mrs. McKenna asked.

"Yeah. I think so."

"What about Mrs. Stone?"

"We'll come back for her."

The two moms crawled out the secret panel on the bottom of the box.

They heard a man screaming and laughing in the darkened wings stage right.

"You fools!"

His voice was dripping evil.

"You weaklings will never stop us!"

"Let's go out the other way," Judy whispered.

Mrs. McKenna nodded.

They ran as quickly and quietly as they could for the stage door on their left.

101

"You weaklings will never stop us!"

Zack recognized the maniac with the meat cleaver from that night on the elevator. The caped madman's shirt and waistcoat were splattered with more blood than he remembered. His top hat nearly flew off his head as he swung his cleaver like an ax and chopped at all the wires and cables snaking up to the table where the stage manager called cues during live performances.

"I'd kill you both, but I have my orders!"

He smashed out a computer monitor.

Of course Mr. Meat Cleaver had chopped the telephone lines first. Slashed right through them with his butcher blade. Smashed the handset with the butt end of his cleaver handle just to make certain nobody would be calling anybody anytime soon.

This was so weird.

The guy was obviously a ghost or a ghoul, so how come he was able to destroy things in the real world?

Zack glanced over at Mr. Kimble, who was quaking in his work boots. He hadn't seen as many spooks as Zack. This was only like his second.

"Where do you keep the jewelry, boy?" the butcher beast snarled at Zack.

Zack thought fast. "Uh, downstairs. There's a big statue made out of gold!"

"Gold?"

Zack nodded. Fast.

The butcher looked like he was drooling when he disappeared.

"Who was he?" asked Kimble.

"Don't know," said Zack.

"He is a demi-devil, a thing of darkness!" said Bartholomew Buckingham as he faded into view.

"Mr. Buckingham," said Zack, "what's going on? That maniac could actually *use* his meat cleaver!"

"The time is out of joint, Zachary! O, cursed spite! That ever you were born to set it right!"

"What?"

"A full moon now rises in the east. In the tug of its gravitational pull, the rules, like the tides, are prone to shift and sway!"

"So tonight, the ghosts can hurt people?"

"Not if you stop them!"

"How?"

"I cannot tell you!"

"*How?*"

Bartholomew swung his arm grandly to the left.

"Seek and ye shall find!"

The scene shop!

102

Grimes ruffled and furled his cape. "Hear me, my loyal and obedient followers! Behold the boy and girl, pure and true!"

He was pointing at Meghan and Derek.

"Meghan?"

"Don't worry, Derek."

"What? Don't worry? They want to kill us."

"Help is on the way."

"Who? They locked up our mothers. Nobody else is in the theater!"

"Zack is."

Derek moaned. "We're dead."

"Silence, boy!" snapped Grimes. Then he turned to face the statue. "Mighty Moloch, we offer unto you, these two children, pure and true!"

Meghan felt the gun in her back again. "Get ready, kid," sneered the thug. "You're almost on."

"Hear me, voracious creator!" Grimes bellowed. "Accept the purest flesh, the sweetest blood! For these two moon children are now ready to depart this earth!"

Oh, no I'm not, thought Meghan.

103

Judy and Mrs. McKenna were in the greenroom—the actors' lounge connected to the dressing rooms backstage.

Judy heard someone scraping at the door that led into the lobby.

Now she heard a bark. A very familiar bark.

Judy pulled open the door.

Zipper jumped up against her legs and was trying to lick her face and bark and jump and lick some more—all at the same time.

"Where's Zack?" Judy asked.

Zipper jumped down. Panted hard. Looked like he was thinking. Sniffed. Once. Twice.

Then he took off.

Back the way Judy and Mary McKenna had just come.

"Let's do this thing!" Grimes barked at Hakeem. "Now!"

"No, Holiness. The portal will not be fully open until the moon is fully risen."

"Blasted curse!"

"Patience, Eminence. Patience. Come with me." Hakeem led Grimes around to the rear of the statue. "See how even now the shroud between this world and the next grows thin?" He pointed to that section of floor squared off by the rotted pillars of the old gallows. The concrete had become translucent and resembled a rippling sheet of wax paper. Grimes could see a whole horde of demons writhing like a bucket of slimy worms beneath his feet.

"Hear me, my people, and listen well! Soon will I lead you all across the threshold of death and restore you to life!"

"Is the boy ready?" snarled a voice from down below. "Will he say the words?"

"What?" Grimes cried imperiously.

"Remember, Reginald," the unknown voice rumbled on, "the boy child must *willingly* recite the Latin script or Moloch will be displeased."

"Bah!" said Grimes. "Which of you demons dares question me?"

"One who knows whereof he speaks," answered Hakeem. "Your grandfather. Professor Nicholas Nicodemus."

105

At Bartholomew Buckingham's suggestion, Zack and Mr. Kimble hurried into the gloomy scene shop.

Looking for . . . well, whatever they were supposed to find.

Kimble tapped Zack on the shoulder. Pointed.

In the middle of the big room, near what looked like a winch coiled with metal cable, Zack saw a short man in baggy pants and suspenders holding his fedora so he could stare down through a hole in the floor without his hat falling into it.

It was the same guy Zack had seen last night tossing sparklers up to Juggler Girl.

"Pietro?" mumbled Mr. Kimble.

The man looked up from the hole. Put the hat on his head.

"Hey! Little Wilbur! How you doin', henh?"

The man had a very thick Italian accent.

"You know this guy?" Zack whispered to Kimble.

"Aya. Used to, anyways. Pietro Bacigalupi. Top special effects man. Back in the 1940s. Died on the job."

The little man shrugged. "There was an accident. Some-body smoked a cigar. Whattaya gonna do?"

"Mr. Bacigalupi was the premiere pyrotechnics wizard of his day," said Kimble. "Smoke pots. Explosions. Canon fire. Whatever a show needed!"

"And Mr. Willowmeier?" said Bacigalupi. "Lemme tell you. The man, he like a nice Fourth of July picnic and fire-works extravaganza. Rockets. Shells. The works. But always remember one thing!" He wagged his finger at Zack. "Safety first!" The finger was a stump and a knuckle.

Bacigalupi looked at the floor again.

"Looks like they got another kind of party goin' on down there. Maybe a barbeque."

Zack noticed that there was a four-by-four square missing from the floor.

"Is that a trapdoor, sir?"

"Sì, sì, sì."

"How'd you open that hatch?"

He shrugged. "I wanted to open it real bad, you know? And guess what? She opened."

Yep. The time and rules were definitely out of joint.

Zack leaned over, peered down through the opening.

Thirty feet below them was the scenery storage room. Zack could see the Minotaur statue. A guy in a turban. Another guy in robes.

Meghan and Derek.

"It's Moloch!" gasped Kimble. "The sacrifice!"

Zack turned to the ghost. "How do you raise and lower scenery to the storage room?"

"In my day," said Bacigalupi, "we used this winch right here."

"Do you know how to operate it, Mr. Kimble?"

"Sure, but . . ."

Zack turned to the dead pyrotechnical wizard. "Mr. Bacigalupi? Did you bring any supplies with you tonight?"

He shrugged. "Not much. Just, you know, some Roman candles, couple sky rockets, some willows, waterfalls, multibreak shells." He tipped his head toward a six-foot-long wooden crate. "Maybe one or two dozen bottle rockets, this very pretty Pandora's blast, some flares, fountains. . . . Not much, really."

Stenciled on the side of the crate was a warning: DAN-GER. *EXTREMELY FLAMMABLE AND EXPLOSIVE.*

"Will they work?" asked Zack.

Bacigalupi shrugged again. "Tonight, they probably work as good as a meat cleaver."

"Give me a hand!" Zack said to Kimble.

The two of them pried the lid off the wooden box.

Then Zack started stuffing his pockets.

106

Reginald Grimes was on his knees, staring at the floor.

"Grandfather?"

"Stand up straight, Reginald," the wizened old man hissed from below.

"How did you get here?"

"The Indian's curse! It summons more demons to this spot than you or I ever could! Hurry, boy! We haven't much time!"

"But—I've never met anyone in my family before!"

"And you never will if you do not complete the resurrection ritual—now!"

"Fear not, Grandfather. I will not fail you."

"Good, because your father certainly did. Stupid, no-good sluggard. Tried to sacrifice his own daughter and son."

"What?"

"You were both born under the full moon. My disciples were too late to save your sister. But Hakeem's father was able to yank you out. Of course, the fire destroyed your arm."

Grimes stared at his withered limb. "My father did this to me?"

"Yes! The imbecile. I was in jail. Heard what he was intending to do. Didn't even have his Tophet set up in the proper place, here at the portal. Rented a warehouse in Danbury. Used toddlers too young to even speak, let alone recite the incantation."

"But . . ."

"Don't worry. He paid for his mistake."

"My father slayed him," said Hakeem, bowing slightly. "Your mother as well."

"Then you people put me in that orphanage. . . ."

"This is your one chance, Reginald!" shouted the professor. "Redeem our family name! You are the only one who can, for you are the sole surviving male heir to our royal bloodline!"

"My father . . . my mother . . ."

"Are both dead! But I can live again. Begin the sacrificial rite!"

107

Sniffing and scampering, Zipper led the way.

Judy and Mrs. McKenna were right behind him. They ran back onto the set, past the ghost lamp, into the wings at stage right.

The monster who had been screaming behind the curtains was, thankfully, gone.

But the stage manager's desk had been demolished.

Zipper sniffed. The desk. The stool. The floor. He circled a few times. Made up his mind. Headed right. Kept running.

Into the scenery shop.

"Zack?" Judy hollered. "Zack?"

"Shhh!"

It was Mr. Kimble. The janitor. He was standing in the center of the shop, slowing uncoiling cable from the drum on a mechanical winch.

"Where's my son?" Judy whispered.

Kimble gestured at the hole in the floor.

108

"Say the words, Derek," Grimes hissed.

Derek coughed. "I can't."

"Say them!"

"Don't, Derek!" Meghan pleaded. "They want to kill us! I don't think they can if you don't say their stupid words."

"Silence, foolish girl! Derek?"

"Yes, sir?" He wheezed.

"My grandfather is counting on me. I am counting on you." He fed him his first line: "*O, magnus Molochus.*"

All Derek could do was hack up another cough.

"Derek?" He could see the rage boiling up in his director's very disappointed face.

"Maybe if you extinguished the charcoal, sir," he suggested. "I'm allergic to smoke."

Zack was descending slowly, sitting in a rope harness attached to the winch line.

Suddenly, he was hit by a spotlight. A follow spot, like they used in musicals so you could see the star better.

Or in prison movies when people tried to escape.

"It's the Jennings boy!" screamed Grimes. "Badir? Jamal? Shoot him!"

Zack threw up his hands. "Wait! Don't shoot! I was born under a full moon, too!"

"What?"

"I was born under a full moon! I would've told you sooner but I just found out. My mother told me."

He heard Derek hacking up a storm.

"Let Derek go. He's too sick to say your words. I'll do it! I'll say it!"

Grimes hesitated.

"*O, magnus Molochus!*" Zack shouted. "See? I almost have the script memorized."

For some reason, Grimes looked at the floor.

Then Zack heard the most hideously grisly voice say, "He will do. He will do just fine."

Judy, Mr. Kimble, and Meghan's mom were kneeling on three sides of the open trapdoor.

Zipper sat on the fourth side.

"What's Zack doing down there?" Judy asked.

"Bein' mighty brave, you ask me," said Mr. Kimble.

She looked around the scene shop. Saw the crate. Read the stenciled warning.

"Then we'd better help him!" She stood up and dragged the box closer to the trapdoor.

Zack pretended he was the one operating the cable, lowering the harness.

"Let Derek go!" he said to Grimes as soon as his feet touched the floor. Or else I'll change my mind."

Again Grimes looked to the floor. "Grandpa?"

Zack could see through the floor. Down below, there was an old man with a purple towel wrapped around his head. The throbbing glow from a fire smoldering under his feet deepened the furrows in his face and made him look terrifying.

"Can I let the other boy go, Grandpa?" Grimes asked.

The demon under the floor sneered up at Derek. He flicked out his tongue. "Fine." He huffed. "Let the coward run away. He won't get far."

"Hey!" Derek protested. Then he heaved a raspy wheeze.

Zack put his hand on Derek's shoulder. "Go upstairs, Derek."

"What? I want to help you guys!"

"You know, I'll never forget when we first met," Zack

said, sounding all choked up. "How you gunned your little truck."

"What?"

"Go upstairs. Play with your truck."

"Are you crazy?"

"Go. Gun. Your truck."

Derek stared at Zack. Zack raised his eyebrows. Twice.

"Oh." Finally. Derek understood what Zack was trying to tell him. "Yeah. My truck. Good idea." He bolted for the open door, running faster than anyone with allergies should be able to.

"How you holding up?" Zack whispered to Meghan.

"This is scary, Zack. They want to toss us on the grill."

"I know. It's what they did to Juggler Girl. Mr. Kimble told me."

"Silence!" Grimes shouted. "We have wasted enough time. The dog moon has risen. It is time for the hounds of hell to rise with it! Say the words."

Zack needed to buy a little more time. Not much. Just enough.

"Hakeem? Hand him the scroll!"

The swarthy man handed Zack a rolled-up tube of ancient papyrus.

"Recite the words!"

Zack adjusted his glasses and dropped the scroll. The brittle document shattered.

"Whoops. Sorry!"

He bent over to pick up the pieces off the floor. Scanned the room. Two guys with guns.

He wished there was only one. They'd have a better chance with just one. Two was going to be tough. He looked up at the trapdoor.

Very tough. Maybe impossible.

"Hurry up, Zack Jennings!" snarled a familiar demon: Mad Dog Murphy. He and his electric chair were under the floor with the others. "I told you I'd be comin' back to get you, boy!"

They'd have one chance. One shot.

"Mr. Jennings?" said Grimes. "Recite the words! Now! Miss McKenna? Prepare to enter the vast unknown!"

"No!" said Meghan. "I won't do it. You can't make me!"

One of the thugs raised his gun, pointed it at Meghan's heart. He cocked the trigger. Zack heard the sharp metallic click.

"Wait!" said Zack. "If you shoot Meghan, Moloch won't get his live human sacrifice!"

"Give me that gun!" Grimes wrestled the revolver out of the muscleman's hand. "The boy's right! The ritual will only work if we exchange their lives for the lives of those down below." He hurled the pistol into the fire pit under the grill.

The gunpowder inside the shells exploded like lethal popcorn. Zack heard five bullets ping against metal.

Good.

Meant they only had one gun now.

"Are you happy, little Miss Movie Star?" Grimes screamed. "Nobody's going to shoot you. We're just going to roast you alive like my father tried to roast me! Like he roasted my sister!"

A sixth bullet exploded.

That was when Zack heard metal start to screech.

Up near the top of the statue.

Near its mouth.

112

"This isn't good," said Judy, peering down at her stepson.

"Hold on," said Kimble. "Steady."

Zipper sank to his belly. Whined.

"Did that statue just move?" asked Mrs. McKenna.

Judy nodded. "This definitely isn't good."

113

A deafening squeal echoed off the walls. Metal twisting and turning against metal. The bull's muzzle creaked open.

"Moloch has girls," rumbled a voice deeper than a canyon at the bottom of the ocean.

Even Grimes seemed amazed.

The statue was talking.

"Have girls. Need boy."

Grimes stepped forward. "You have girls?"

The bull's head nodded once with a thunderous clatter.

"The child my grandfather sacrificed. Plus my sister?"

Another cacophony of clanking as the beast nodded again.

"So you only need the boy?"

Another earth-trembling nod. "Feed me the one called Zack. Need boy."

With that, the bull became silent.

"I'm going down there!" said Mr. Kimble. He stood up, clutched the cable.

"I'm going with you," said Meghan's mom.

"Wait," said Judy.

"Zack needs our help!" said Kimble.

"Well," said Judy, as calmly as she could, "I think we might have a better *shot* at helping him from up here."

With that, she handed each of them something from the wooden box.

"Wait till Zack gives us the signal!"

Zipper barked.

He wasn't waiting. He took off running.

"Let Meghan go!" shouted Zack. "You don't need her anymore."

"No, Zack. I'm staying here with you."

"Meghan, it isn't safe."

"Zack?"

"Get out of here!"

Grimes flung up his crippled arm. "You heard the boy! Go! Leave! My sister died so you might live!"

Meghan gave Zack a confused look.

He nodded toward the sliding steel doors. "My glasses have sports lenses."

"What?"

"They're like safety goggles. *You'll* be better off behind those big steel doors. In case, you know, the sparks start flying when I hit the fire."

Meghan nodded like she understood. She ran over to the open doors. Hid behind them.

"Where's my grandfather?" Grimes spun around, stared at the floor. "Where'd he go?"

"He's fading," said Hakeem. "They are all fading. We must begin!"

Badir and Jamal stepped forward. Jamal raised his revolver. Aimed it at Zack's head. "Say the words, boy!"

"And do not worry about climbing up," added Badir. "We are going to throw you!"

Zack closed his eyes. Took in a deep breath. Shook out his fingers. Took in another breath.

"Mr. Jennings?" said Grimes. "Now!"

"I need to focus on the words."

"Now!"

"Hey, Zack!" It was Derek. Behind him. Breathing heavy. "I'm back."

It was showtime.

Zack stepped toward the statue.

"O, *magnus Molochus!*"

"Excellent!" said Grimes.

"*Nos duo vitam nostram damus ut vos omnes qui huc arcessiti estis vivatis.*"

"He memorized it so quickly! Go on, boy! Go on!"

Zack moved close enough to hear the brass statue creak and warble as its heated metal began to expand.

"*Puer et puella . . .*"

"Go on!" urged Grimes.

"*Puri et fideles . . .*"

"Pure and true, yes, yes!"

"*Morimur . . .*"

"You die!"

"*Ut vos resuscitet.*"

"That they may be resurrected! He said it. He said it all!"

The fire and Grimes roared and cackled.

Zzzzzzzzzzzzzzzz.

Zack finally heard the sound he'd been hoping to hear: an annoying mosquito with a microphone. The nasal whine of Derek Stone's tweaked-out monster truck flying across the floor.

Thwack!

That was the second sound Zack had hoped to hear: the remote-controlled truck slamming into Badir's ankles like it had slammed into his!

Clunk!

Sound three. Badir dropping his gun.

Now Zack reached into his pockets and grabbed two fistfuls of fireworks.

He tossed them into the fire pit.

The Fourth of July started shooting out the bull's nostrils and up through its chimney horns.

"I've got the gun!" screamed Derek.

"Heave it in the fire!"

Derek tossed the weapon into the blaze just as another sky rocket blasted off. This one streaked straight up, whistled into the exhaust hood, and screeched through the ductwork like a mortar shell until, Zack was certain, it exploded into a shower of cascading sparks right over the roof of the Hanging Hill Playhouse.

"I'm going upstairs to rescue my mom!" Derek shouted.

"Hurry!" said Zack.

As Derek ran out the doors, Grimes lurched toward Zack.

"You insolent child!" he howled.

Then Zack heard an even louder howl. A cat?

Now a bark! Zipper.

Grimes dropped to his knees, held open his arms. "Jinx?"

A hell cat the size of a beaver came charging out of the shadows with Zipper in hot pursuit. The giant cat looked ready to claw somebody's eyes out.

It yowled, then leapt up at Grimes. Clung on to his head. The madman looked like he was wearing a fur face mask.

"Fire away!" Zack screamed to Judy. "Fire!"

Judy was a pretty good shot with the bottle rockets.

Mrs. McKenna, too.

But it was a good thing Meghan was hiding behind the blast doors. Some of the moms' misguided missiles spiraled around the room like out-of-control comets.

Mr. Kimble? He had juggled knives when he was a kid. He still had the stuff.

He nailed the screaming, cat-wrestling Grimes in the butt with a lumbo whistling starburst rocket. So on top of the wild caterwauling, Zack now heard tuxedo pants sizzling.

Next Kimble tagged Hakeem with a plastic-tipped missile in the side of his felt hat. Flaming embers spewed up and made it look like the poor guy was taking a sparkle shower underneath a rainbow-colored Niagara Falls.

Badir and Jamal ran out the doors.

Judy and Mrs. McKenna tossed down more rockets, the kinds that made starbursts and lots of *siss-boom-bang* noises up in the sky. Zack hurled them all into Moloch's fire so his hollowed-out horns would keep shooting off distress signals like the big finale in a fireworks show.

Hey, if you couldn't call the cops, sometimes it was a smart idea to send up a flare.

The crazed cat had vanished but Mr. Grimes's face was a scratched and bloody mess. Zack guessed the full moon meant ghost claws were real for the night, too.

"Let me assist you, Exalted One." Hakeem—his hat fried, his hair scorched—limped over to where Grimes teetered to his feet. "Do not despair. We shall try again, next August . . ."

Now Zack heard the whoosh he had heard last night in the elevator.

"I won't go back!"

The butcher with the meat cleaver materialized in front of Grimes.

"I won't go back!" Suddenly, he stopped ranting and stared at Grimes's turban.

"Is that an emerald?"

Grimes nodded.

"Give it to me!"

"Never!" Grimes tried to roar. "Return below, foolish demon. I summoned you hence. Now I command you to depart!"

"I will not depart without that shiny green jewel!"

"Return below! I command you!"

The demon laughed. "You cannot command me to do anything!"

"I am the lord high priest of . . ."

"Careful!" warned Hakeem. "Remember: Those summoned can quickly turn against the summoner."

This one sure did.

He swung his meat cleaver like an executioner's ax and lopped off the high priest's head, sending the precious emerald and the turban and Reginald Grimes's skull rolling across the concrete floor like a bloody, free-kicked soccer ball. It stopped at Hakeem's feet.

Another whoosh, a tormented scream, and the demon butcher was sucked down into the concrete floor. He disappeared. His cleaver clunked to the ground. The thing remained real. The man did not.

Now Hakeem picked up his high priest's head, cradled it to his chest, and began to blubber.

"He was the last of his royal line! Our final hope! I must bring him back to life! I must resurrect the high priest of Ba'al!"

He turned to the statue.

"Take me, Moloch! I will be the boy! Take me!" And he began the incantation: *"O, magnus Molochus. . . ."*

Zack closed his eyes.

He didn't want to see this.

"Aaaiiieeeee!"

He heard a whomp! A roar of flames. Horrible screams. Shrieks.

Hakeem had willingly leapt into the fire.

Zack kept his eyes closed.

Until he heard what sounded like a disgusted burp, the roaring clatter of brass, and a very queasy groan.

"Oooh."

Zack dared to peek up at the statue.

The Minotaur looked like he might puke.

"Bad boy," urped the statue. "Very, very bad."

Hakeem must not have been pure *or* true.

At long last, Zack heard sirens in the distance.

117

It took several hours for Judy and Mrs. McKenna to explain to the police and firefighters what had happened.

And what they told the officers wasn't a complete lie.

Hakeem had, in a way, killed Grimes. Calling him Exalted One. Making him think he was more special than anybody in the world. Because Hakeem's charred carcass was discovered clutching Grimes's skull inside the doused fire pit and because the police had the murder weapon (the meat cleaver) it was pretty much an open-and-shut case: murder/suicide.

Paramedics rolled Mrs. Stone on a gurney to an ambulance parked in front of the Hanging Hill Playhouse. She was still conked out.

"I'm riding with her to the hospital," said Derek.

"Thanks for coming back," said Zack.

"Yeah," said Meghan. "Thanks! That was extremely brave."

"Sorry," Derek said with a wink. "Can't do an autograph now. Catch me later!" He hopped into the back of the ambulance. Zipper barked to say goodbye. "Catch you later, Zip!"

"I'll call the scrap metal folks first thing in the morning," said Mr. Kimble, who was standing on the porch with Zack, Judy, Meghan, and Mrs. McKenna. "Have 'em cart away the brass statue. Melt it down to make buttons. Door knockers."

It was nearly midnight when the last official vehicle finally pulled out of the gravel parking lot.

Meghan came over to where Zack stood and kissed him.

"Zack Jennings," she whispered, "you're my hero!" While Zach was totally stunned, Sassakus showed up on the front lawn.

118

The noble Native American ruler materialized accompanied by his daughter, Princess Nepauduckett.

She wasn't crying anymore. In fact, she looked happy.

The towering chieftain gestured for Zack to come down and join him on the dewy patch of grass. Zack did. Meghan and the adults followed him down the porch steps.

"Do you know who I am?" the apparition asked.

"I think so."

"You're Sassakus!" said Mrs. McKenna, the history buff.

"I cursed this land because I knew white men to be demons. They accused my daughter of stealing corn. They executed her here on Hangman's Hill." When Sassakus stepped forward, his necklace of shells rattled like a skeleton's tambourine. "But I have seen what you have done this day. Why did you take the other boy's place?"

"I don't know, sir," Zack answered honestly. "It just seemed like the right thing to do at the time. I wanted to help."

Sassakus nodded thoughtfully. "You are not like the others. You are not a demon. You are the demon slayer?"

"Maybe. I don't know. I just wanted to help out the good guys." Zack turned around to point up at the moonlit theater building and wasn't at all surprised to see that, once again, a whole host of ghostly actors and stagehands were crowded in the glowing windows on all five floors—even up in every turret and tower.

"You are special, Zack Jennings, yes?"

"He is," said Judy, standing behind Zack, placing her hands on his shoulders. "Very special."

"Very well." Sassakus clapped his hands. "The ones below are banished forever. I remove my curse and forgive the evil done unto my daughter, for I do not wish that same evil to rule my soul for all eternity."

For a second, Zack wondered if Sassakus was talking about the kind of evil done to Zack by his mother, Susan Potter. Maybe she had tried to help him. Maybe she had shown up back at the hotel to protect him from Mad Dog Murphy. It was a possibility.

So was it time for him to forgive her?

Time to move forward without constantly looking back?

Maybe. Maybe not. Hey, it took Sassakus what? Four-hundred some years. Zack might need a little more time, too.

"Come, daughter. We must move on."

"Where to?"

"Someplace much happier. Our time here is ended."

With that, they disappeared.

"Huzzah!" the phantom actors shouted from every window. "Huzzah!"

"Attaboy, Zachary!" shouted Mr. Willowmeier from way up in the highest tower. Zack heard two girls giggle. He figured Mr. Willowmeier was throwing another one of his famous cast parties.

"So many," said Kimble.

"Can you see them, Mom?" Meghan asked.

"Yes, dear. How could I not?"

Wilbur Kimble shook his head in awe. "So, so many."

"Mr. Kimble?"

"Aya?"

"Well, sir, I finally saw my dead mother today."

"Is that so?"

"Yes, sir. I think it's because I really, truly believe I wasn't the one who made her miserable or killed her. The same way *you* didn't kill your sister."

"I suppose not."

"Hey, I just met the guy who *did*. He should change his name from Professor Nicodemus to Doctor Nutjob."

"I just wish I could've stopped him."

"You were ten years old!"

"Aya."

"Plus, you didn't have any pyrotechnical devices or an ace gunner covering your back!"

"You're right. Nicodemus killed Clara. Not me."

"I think Clara agrees."

"You do, do you?"

Zack smiled. "But don't take my word. Ask her yourself."

Kimble turned around and saw what Zack had already seen; his sister, standing on the porch, juggling six spinning balls high above her head.

"Clara?"

"Hello, Wilbur! It's wonderful to see you again!"

As Mr. Kimble wiped away a tear and went up the steps to join his sister, Judy came over to Zack and gestured toward the building. "So, Zack. Is your mother up there?"

Zack shook his head. "Nope. She's standing right next to me."

"I meant your real mother."

"I know. Me too."

When Zack said that, Judy kissed him, too.

Acknowledgments

I want to thank my incredible editor, R. Schuyler Hooke, who truly knows how to help a writer find the story buried underneath all the words.

Elizabeth Mackey Johnson, Lisa McClatchy, Jenny Madden, and all the wonderful people at Random House who treat their authors so well.

My agent, Eric Myers.

My incredible wife, cheerleader, and first reader, J.J.—you should hear her do all the voices!

Meghan, Sam, Rodman John, Anna, Riley, Maddie, Wendell, Wesley, Timothy, and all my other early readers.

Our gray cat Parker, who so graciously posed for me during the creation of Jinx.

Our dog, Fred, who is a big Zipper and a constant inspiration. I'm so glad he had to do his business that one time at three a.m.

And most especially, I'd like to thank all the teachers, students, parents, and librarians who have taken Zack and Judy into their hearts and homes. You guys are the best.

Chris Grabenstein is the author of *The Crossroads*, which *Booklist* called a "rip-roaring ghost story" in its starred review, as well as six critically acclaimed adult mysteries and thrillers. In fact, his first book, *Tilt-A-Whirl*, won the Anthony Award for best first mystery. If any of that sounds like a TV commercial, maybe it's because Chris wrote copy for TV and radio ads for too, too long. He also wrote for Jim Henson's Muppets and co-wrote the CBS TV movie *The Christmas Gift*, starring John Denver. Right out of college, Chris did improvisational comedy with some of the top performers in New York City, including one guy named Bruce Willis. Chris and his wife, J.J., live in Manhattan with three cats and a dog named Fred, who starred on Broadway in *Chitty Chitty Bang Bang*. You can visit Chris and go behind the scenes of *The Hanging Hill* at www.ChrisGrabenstein.com.